T0156898

The Marshall of
SANTA FE

RALPH GATLIN

WESTBOW
PRESS
A DIVISION OF THOMAS NELSON
& ZONDERVAN

WestBow Press books may be ordered through booksellers or by contacting:

WestBow Press
A Division of Thomas Nelson & Zondervan
1663 Liberty Drive
Bloomington, IN 47403
www.westbowpress.com
1 (866) 928-1240

ISBN: 978-1-4908-8223-9 (sc)
ISBN: 978-1-4908-8224-6 (hc)
ISBN: 978-1-4908-8222-2 (e)

Library of Congress Control Number: 2015908647

Print information available on the last page.

WestBow Press rev. date: 05/28/2015

This book is dedicated to my family, my beautiful wife, Jane, and to our children and their spouses. They are Mark and Melissa, Wade and Linda, and Amy and Mike. It is dedicated also to our grandchildren, Anna Ruth, Alyson, Andrew, Wesley, Peter, Madison, Joshua, and Jane Ann. God (Ussen) has been very generous to us.

Ralph Gatlin, the eighty-two-year-old author of two previous books, *Lone Eagle—The White Apache* and *The White Apache Returns Home*, has led an active life. He has fished in Alaska, Canada, and Mexico. He rafted the Chattooga River and flew in a hot-air balloon over the Serengeti plains in Africa.

Prologue

I was the marshal of Santa Fe. It had calmed down. Most of the troublemakers went on down the road to Albuquerque or up to Taos. Needless to say, the business owners were not happy with the money I had cost them.

Susan and I had been married for about four years. Mary Estes, Susan's mother, had sold us the hotel and moved back to Virginia, where her two widowed sisters lived. I was betting that Mary moved back to Santa Fe soon. She was accustomed to more excitement in her life now.

My dad and mom (Sam and Jane Davis) were doing well. Dad's love of having his own land and Mom's involvement in the planning of Beth and Cowboy's wedding in the spring had given them both a real purpose in life. I'd give them my half of the ranch Cowboy and I owned together when they got married. Nate had married a daughter of one of Don Luis's vaqueros. She was truly an olive-skinned beauty. Don Luis had given them twenty-five thousand acres and helped them build a cabin on it.

Nana was the only chief of Victorio's tribe who was still living. He and two hundred of his warriors lived and raided the Mexicans in the Province Of Senora, Mexico. They did not harm settlers in the United States. Nana didn't want our army after him.

One surprising outcome in all of this was that Nana kept at least one of his braves roving Dad's land, always looking out for Dad, Mom, and Beth. He truly liked and respected the Davis family. Having me as his blood brother helps Nana make the decision to watch over them.

Times had changed. Most of the ones who had trained me to be a warrior, including Quannah, Chato, White Killer, the Shaman, and Serpentino, had gone to the other world of good hunting, sunshine, friends, and relatives. It was different now. Some Apache had begun to lose some of their pride and honor as time passed. Nothing good could come out of losing their honor. While the Indians were always dangerous in the desert, it was the gunfighters who were dangerous in the towns.

I was about to face the biggest challenge of my life.

The Comanche, under their new chief, Grizzly Killer, had left their Fort Stanton reservation and had to be brought in. The Comanche had left because Sauktauk, their old chief and my blood brother, had been pushed into a fight with soldiers at the reservation and been killed.

Ron Jedrokoski, who stood six foot three and was 280 pounds of muscle and meanness, was back in my life. Ron's father and mother had died in a worldwide flu epidemic, and he'd had to work on the dock under a man who had beat him every day. It had made him mean and mad. He'd killed Abe and joined the army. In an encounter with him, I had beat him up so badly that I'd crippled him, and he'd had to leave the army. He wanted to kill my family and me.

Last, but not the least of my problems, was Tim Dukes, thought by some to be the fastest gun in the West. He was on his way to Santa Fe to kill me. It was going to be interesting. It was up to Ussen now. The war between the States had been over for eighteen years, and many of the hardy survivors had come west. They'd had their souls tested in the great conflict and wanted more for themselves and their families.

They'd found the ten inches of rain a year the desert land got was not even adequate enough to have drinking water. All the major towns had been growing quickly with the influx of uneducated laborers coming west. Too many of them had no other way to make a living, so they became outlaws. They had no honor. They sold their souls and guns to the highest bidder. The towns grew. Santa Fe was no exception. It had grown to over five thousand inhabitants.

Sheriffs were hired by the towns to keep law and order. The marshals were appointed by the federal judges. The law officers had their hands full protecting the people.

Law enforcement was a dangerous profession. So was being an Indian. The Indians were being exterminated. The same land set aside for the Apache was often also given to homesteaders. The land was only good for ranches with thousands of acres. It took at least one hundred acres of the barren land to support one steer. They also needed deep springs or small streams on their land to make it productive. Most settlers still believed the only good Indian was a dead one. The Indians, threatened constantly by the homesteaders, had to leave or fight. It was a fight they couldn't win. Justice still favored the homesteaders. Either way, the land reverted back to the government. The US Army almost always took the side of the settlers over the Indians in any dispute over the titles to the land.

In the late 1880s, the Apache were fewer than two thousand. Half of these Apache lived out in the desert of northern Mexico and raided down around Senora, Mexico. They knew they had to come into the Fort Apache Reservation soon, or Victorio's tribe would be gone forever.

The Apache could never forgive nor forget how the Mexicans had poisoned the whiskey given to the warriors in trade. The poison had killed over fifty warriors. Then the Mexicans had killed the women and children, over one hundred of them. They had scalped men, women, and children and sold the scalps to the governor of Senora, Mexico.

Geronimo, their greatest war chief, had surrendered. He did not have to stay on a reservation since he was a good friend of Lieutenant Gatewood and General Crook.

The Indian tribes were slowly but surely being rounded up and put on reservations. Anyone not coming was forced to do so, or they would be killed or imprisoned. Some of the more fierce warriors in Victorio's tribe would rather be killed. They did not have a real choice. They had the rest of the tribe to take care of. All of them would finally come in. A lot of them had become scouts for the US Army. They were totally faithful, and Congress later had authorized a special medal for them.

Custer was dead. Most of the Seventh Calvary had died with him. They had chased one hundred Sioux over the side of a mountain (Little Bighorn) that had thirty-five thousand more of the Lakota Sioux waiting for them on the other side. The Battle of Little Bighorn, or its more descriptive name of "Custer's Last Stand," was the only clear-cut major victory the Indians had won over the US Army. A few small patrols had escaped the ambush. Most of them hadn't. Over a thousand of the Sioux had escaped to Canada. After a couple of years, they had returned to the United States. Most of them had been put on a reservation in the Black Hills of Dakota near Rapid City, where the discovery of gold would again create problems for them and the US government. Most of the Indians would have to leave the Black Hills. There were still productive gold mines in Deadwood and Lead, South Dakota, today.

Chief Sitting Bull had been made a star in Buffalo Bill's Wild West Show. Chief Joseph and his Nez Pierce had decided, "We will fight no more." They had traveled 1,350 miles, pursued by the US Army. They had never been caught. They had just gotten tired of running. The Cherokee Indians had finished their "Trail of Tears."

The Seminoles had fought three wars with the US Army and had never surrendered. They had just disappeared into the

Everglades, a swamp in Florida, where no army could follow. The Blackfeet, Kiowa, Navajo, Seneca, Mohawk, and over seventy-five other tribes were caught in a net that was getting smaller and smaller. There was only one thing to do: go on the Indian reservations.

It was the gunmen who now controlled most of the West. It was the era of the gunfighters. Some of the fastest gun fighters were Wyatt Earp, Doc Holliday, Wes Harden, Bill Tighman, Jim Ringgold, Johnny DeHane, the Clantons, Clay Allison, Bill Bonney (a.k.a. Billy the Kid), Bat Masterson, Tom Bell, Sam Bass, Tim Dukes, and many others.

It was also the time of a few large gangs of outlaws who thought they were bigger than the law or the US government. They thought they were safe because of their large numbers. This would change in the near future. The town marshal and the sheriff were considered fair targets. Some towns hired gunfighters to be their sheriffs. In a short period of time, it was the sheriff who owned the town.

Phoenix, Arizona, had one such marshal. My old enemy Ron Jedrokoski was the marshal, and he controlled Phoenix. He had started as a sheriff and bribed a federal judge to make him a marshal.

It was late October 1884. God (Ussen) had been good to Susan and me. We were very happy. I had not changed. The major beliefs of my life given to me by my two families were still the same. I was still more Apache than I was a settler. I believed Psalm 23 showed that Ussen and God were one and the same, as evident from this combination of the English version and the Native American version of Psalm 23.

The great Father above is a shepherd chief. I am his, and with him, I want not.
He throws out to me a rope,
And the name of the rope is love,

And he draws me to where the grass is green
And the water not dangerous,
And I eat and am satisfied.

Sometimes my heart is very weak
And falls down,
But he lifts me up again
And draws me into a good road.
His name is wonderful.

Sometimes—and it may not be very soon;
It may be very long, long in time—
He will draw me into a valley.
It is dark there, but I'll be afraid not,
For it is between those mountains
That the shepherd creator will meet me,
And the hunger that I have in my heart
All through this life will be satisfied.

He gives me a staff to lean upon.
He spreads a table before me
With all kinds of food.
He puts his hand upon my head
And all the "tired" is gone.
My cup he fills until it runs over.
What I tell is true.
I lie not.

These roads that are a ways ahead
Will stay with me through life and after,
And afterward, I will go to live
In the big tepee and sit down
With the shepherd chief forever.

My philosophy was still quite simple. It went back to Ussen (God), who was our maker and the God of nature. It was also doing what was right. Personal honor was everything. Sometimes in a major battle, a dog soldier (Serpintino) would drive a stake into the ground in the hottest part of the battle. He would tie himself to the stake and stay there until the battle was won or he was killed. When a warrior did this, the battle stopped long enough for both sides to clasp their fists to their chests as a salute to honor the dog soldiers. If a man did not have honor, he had nothing. I was about to become a dog soldier and drive my stake into the ground.

McGregor, the mercantile storeowner, and Jake, the shrunken owner of the livery stables, were still happy with me. McGregor was a totally honest, tough, middle-aged man whom everyone respected and had faith in. Jake's claims to fame were that he had a big voice for such a shrunken body and could spit a stream of tobacco juice ten feet and pin a fly to the wall. No one had ever seen him miss. These two made most of the decisions about Santa Fe. They made good ones so I didn't have to worry about it.

The merchants would soon change their minds. Trouble was coming back to Santa Fe.

CHAPTER 1

Tim Dukes

I put on the short deerskin coat that was made for me by an Apache woman who keeps an eye on my Apache clothes and me. She was one of the few left who made the deer skins the same as in the old days. Waterproof, warm clothes were hard to find. I turned out the kerosene lamp in the foyer of the hotel before stepping out onto the front porch. The hotel had the slight odor of kerosene and old age—it was a friendly smell. It was a good smell to me. It was said that the wood in the front part of our hotel came from an early pony-express building that had never been finished since the coming of the railroad and the telegraph had put the pony express out of business.

I slid away from the door even though the door was painted black. I learned a long time ago from the Apache that it was never wise to stand in any place that you could be targeted. In this case, the door itself would bracket me. I started to step out on the wooden sidewalk.

I had that feeling on the back of my neck again. I unbuttoned the short deerskin coat I had just finished buttoning. I pushed it back from my pistol and slid the gun up and down in its holster so it wouldn't stick. My sixth sense told me someone who wanted to kill me was standing across the street, waiting for me. The Apache

1

called the sixth sense "a gift from Ussen," which was their name for God. I'd discovered I had it while living with Victorio and his Apaches after being captured by them. The shaman (Apache medicine man), Loren, Victorio's warrior sister, and Geronimo all had it. Mine was the strongest. I stood perfectly still, knowing my eyes would detect motion, even as dark as it was.

It was only a few minutes before the sun would begin its relentless march across the sky. It was uncomfortably cold but not as cold as it was going to be.

Sure enough, the man standing on the wooden sidewalk across the street shifted his weight from one foot to the other. I knew for sure where he was now. I could kill him real easy from here, but my honor wouldn't let me.

I still had that feeling. This man was dangerous. The sheriff of Durango, Colorado, had wired me that Tim Dukes was the fastest gunman he had ever seen. All my senses went on full alert. It looked like I was going to find out how fast Tim was. I did not worry about it.

The first rays of the sun struck the top of our two-story building behind me. The building was a hotel, restaurant, and boarding house. It was still too dark to recognize him, but my senses told me he was the one named Tim Dukes who was planning to kill me. I knew it was already settled in his mind since he had been standing out here in the cold weather, waiting for me to come out.

This was the time the Apaches called "the killing time." It was their favorite time to attack their enemies. They also called it "the dying time" since the mortally wounded, the elderly, and the terminally sick chose this time to die. This came from an old Apache story passed down for hundreds of years. It was the story of how the Apache began. It had been told word for word from father to son for many centuries.

Victorio had told it to me, and one day, I would tell it to my sons. The wind came from the great mountains north of Santa Fe, bringing its fingers of the ice-cold air with it.

I already knew a lot about the silhouette across the street. He was an honorable man. He had not tried to ambush me. He was a confident man. He knew I could see him, and it didn't bother him.

I checked my jacket again. I didn't want it to catch and slow down my draw. These were the things gunfighters did automatically if they wanted to live. I had already made sure my gun was even with my fingertips.

I wouldn't have to reach down very far to get to it. All I'd have to do was shoot as I brought it up. It would save only a split second, but that was the difference between life and death in my business. A lot of dead cowboys didn't check their guns regularly or learn that you point your pistol just like you point your finger. You had to make the first shot count. You might not get another one.

I walked toward the jail. It was on the side of the street where the man was standing. The sun would be in my eyes soon. It was a smart move.

It was light enough now to tell that he was the man who had come into town yesterday.

I walked toward him. We were now twenty feet apart.

My Apache name was the Lone Eagle, the White Apache. It was a name given to me by Ussen. The settlers called him "God." There didn't seem to be any difference in Ussen and God. The difference was only in the people who believed in them. Both of them were the same one who made the world and gave us the mountains, the prairies, the deserts, and the lifesaving waters. He was the God of nature.

I was given my name on one of the peaks in the Sandia Mountains in a driving rainstorm with lightning striking all around me. Ussen had sent a golden eagle to perch beside me on the ledge I was sitting on. A voice either in my head or out loud had said, "You are now the Lone Eagle, the White Apache. You are equal parts settler and Apache. You will have to walk a path between the two people, making decisions only you can make. You will live in honor and truth the rest of your life. You have earned the name the Lone Eagle. You will earn your name every day. It is the way of the warrior."

The chill on the back of my neck continued. I pushed my coat away from my gun again. I always kept my gun fully loaded. Even the chamber under the firing pin was loaded. Some people left it empty because they believed it kept the gun from going off accidentally. Gunfighters had more to worry them than an accidental shot. They needed the small difference in time. Some even filed the firing pin down to make it faster at striking the bullet. Now that was dangerous. Any kind of jolt might make the gun go off.

The rays of the sun now touched half of our building. A little more, and the sun would be in my eyes. It was brighter on the side of the street where I was standing. The sun's rays were now light enough for us to recognize each other.

Tim was smooth faced and neat and impressed everyone with his quiet, Southern manners while eating at the hotel. Susan had made a comment about him.

Some might think good manners are a sign of weakness, like Cherokee Bob of Durango had. I don't! Cherokee Bob had discovered it the hard way.

I knew Tim was really fast with a gun. I was going to find out just how fast he was. It was good to fight the best. He had not sold his soul to the Devil. If I stayed a marshal, sooner or later, someone would beat me. I did not worry about it. Ussen would decide whether I lived or died. I didn't plan to be a marshal forever. One day, I would quit and become a rancher. I knew you couldn't beat all of them all the time. Sometimes you had to be just plain lucky.

CHAPTER 2

The Gunfight

I believe that Ussen had led me here, and whatever happened now was the way it should be. The ranchers of Mexico, the United States, and the townspeople had to enforce the laws and face the gunmen themselves if they didn't have their own lawman.

I had been wounded a couple of times before by Black Jack Ketchem, who might have become a king in the New Mexico territory if he and I had not fought a duel in the main street of Santa Fe at high noon. I had been hit twice in my right leg. He hadn't survived.

It looked like we had a similar problem. This time, I might have Ron Jedrokoski, who was 280 pounds of muscle and meanness, and his seventy-five member outlaw gang against me.

Santa Fe was where I'd met Susan, and I knew she was the only one for me. I was not going to leave it or her.

I knew I should not give Tim Dukes a chance. Then my Apache honor and curiosity came in. A fierce enemy makes for an enjoyable fight.

I wished I could sit down with him and talk about our differences. We might resolve them.

He stopped his walk. He was now in position with the sun in my eyes. I squinted and looked to the left of him. The sun was not as bright there. I could see his outline clearly. It didn't really matter. I knew where my bullets would go. I was ready.

He said to me, "You are Tom Davis, the marshal of Santa Fe?" as if he was in great thought.

"Yes I am. What can I do for you?"

"My name is Tim Dukes. I have one question for you. Did you leave my brother Rodney out in the desert to die?"

"No, I gave him a chance to live. He chose a way to die by being a member of a gang that tried to steal a herd we were driving to Abilene, Kansas. He was a coward."

"I gave all of the survivors the option of the desert or hanging. They all chose the desert. Each of them was given a canteen full of water. I don't know if you know this or not, but your brother was the meanest man in the gang. One of the two men who survived the desert works at the Lazy Corral Bar up the street. You can talk to him if you want to. Your brother tried to steal what little water the eight men had and slip away from them. Again, he chose a way to die. He signed his own death warrant when they caught him stealing the water. They did not give him any water to drink after that."

The sidewalk was covered with sand that the wind moved back and forth to wherever it wished. It made little mounds of sand. Then it blew them away, and it started all over again. It would go on forever.

Tim knew I was probably right. His brother was mean.

Tim is ready to begin the gunfight and yells, "Draw!" Without knowing why, Tim hesitates. His eyes contract slightly, and we both start at the same time. This alone could have secured his death but I allow it. All of my senses explode.

As he draws his pistol, one of his long spurs becomes entangled in a crack on the wooden sidewalk. It turns him slightly away from me.

I was a split second behind him. I had to increase my speed, or be killed. I relaxed and allowed my reflexes take over. It helped.

I increased the speed of my draw by being smoother. I could tell that we were about even now. Both guns went off at the same time. It sounded like one shot.

He almost beat me. We are both fast, quick on the draw. He had a small advantage since he'd started the gunfight. I felt a burning sensation on the side of my head. His bullet had cut a narrow furrow there. My bullet hit the barrel of his pistol, making it explode. Fragments of this gun flew all over him. Pieces of the shattered gun cut his right arm, leg, and hip. Both of us are bleeding profusely. The young man stood straight up, waiting for me to kill him. Most gunmen would have done so. They wouldn't have to face Tim again. He didn't beg for his life. He didn't look like he was afraid to die either.

"Go ahead and finish it."

I didn't want to kill him. "Don't be too eager to die. I have some questions to ask you."

I decided to wait until Doc tended to his wounds to find out why someone would want him to kill me.

I might put Tim in jail for a day or so, time enough to let his wounds heal since none of them were serious and maybe he'd tell me all he knew. I believed that if Tim felt right about me, he'd tell me the truth. I might just let him go free. I was leaning toward that. His word would be good.

I said, "Doc will fix you up. My deputy will bring you back to the jail."

I hoped I would never have to find out who was the fastest between Tim and me. It was that close. I almost had made the cardinal mistake. I'd misjudged my opponent. Pete, my deputy, who had been inside the jail for only a few minutes, and Joshua, who had spent the night in the jail, came running out of the jail with their pistols drawn. Andrew, the third brother, was off for several days. He was a spelunker. (He spent some time off exploring caves in the area.) Some of them were pretty big. The deputies were relieved to see everyone standing up. Joshua was more relieved than Pete because he had to bury the losers. He thought I had been ambushed.

Joshua was one of the three brothers working as my deputies. Anna Ruth was the first female attorney in Santa Fe. She held her own with the male attorneys. She was older than Pete, Joshua, and Andrew. Joshua was glad that Tim and I were still standing. He didn't have to clean up the mess and get Doc to declare us dead. He didn't have to take us out to Boot Hill and dig a hole in the almost frozen ground. After a few more days, he would have to dig in frozen soil. It had always been Pete's job until Joshua had joined my deputies. We had buried a few so-called gunfighters in Santa Fe's Boot Hill. Some fools even rushed to go there. Trouble in Santa Fe had gone down. Some of the merchants had lost a lot of business and, consequently, a lot of money. Money changed things. I believed they were about ready for me to resign. I'd had some thoughts on that too.

I told Pete, "Take this young man over to Doc Jordan, tell him to fix him up, and I will pay for it. Also, tell him he might need to look at my head when he is through with this man. Bring Tim back with you."

I looked at Tim, and another face popped up. He and his brother, Rodney, did resemble each other in their faces but not in their behavior. The face of Rodney Dukes popped into my head. I remembered the young man vividly. He had been full of anger and venom, not for what he had done or wanted to do, but because he had not killed some of us when they had tried to steal our herd. There seemed to be all the difference in the world in the two brothers. I'd bet Rodney had been in trouble all his life, and I would bet also that Tim had spent a lot of his life getting him out of trouble. I waved them on over to Doc James. Doc had heard the shots and had already gotten his medical bag ready. He knew it would require his services.

Doc was the doctor, the dentist, the vet, and the mortician. I took my bandanna off and tied it on my head. It put pressure on the wound. It stopped most of the bleeding.

The air was crisp and cold. The pleasant wind in the summer brought a needed coolness with it. It was soft and pleasant. It turned into a killing wind in the winter. It brought death and starvation to the Indian tribes who were not lucky enough to stock up for the winter. It was strange that the Apache would not stock up fish for the winter or eat them unless they were starving. It had something to do with an old Indian legend. The cold mountain wind whirling around me found the places where I didn't have enough clothes on. It was the middle of October, and we should have had a lot of snow by now. We were having an unusually late fall. However, I could smell snow in the air. Sometime soon, we would have a real snowstorm and not the light dusting of powder snow that painted the peaks of the Sangre de Christo (Blood of Christ) Mountains. The real winter was about to begin.

One of the first permanent buildings in Santa Fe was a church with a statue of Jesus adorning the back wall of the Catholic Church built by the Spanish explorers in the early 1500s. The church would one day be famous as the oldest church in America that had never had its doors closed. It had always been open to everyone. It was still active. The Spaniards usually had a monk with them. There was nothing soft about the Catholicism brought in by the Spaniards. The town's architecture definitely was Spanish, Anglo, and Indian. It was a mixture of adobe and wood buildings. Wooden sidewalks were covered with sand that the wind used to paint pictures, but it blew the sand away almost as fast as it painted them. The sidewalks varied in height, but the sand blown by the wind evened them out. Santa Fe was a combination of two cities, as were most towns in the West. One part of the town was generally known as "the other side of the tracks" or the red-light district. The Palace Saloon, on the other side of the street, was in the red-light district, while the hotel on this side of the street was in the good part of town. The two sections had a total of over 4,900 people in them. Most of them lived on the right side of the tracks. The upper part of town was supposedly the better class of people. I had not seen a lot of the better class of people. They were only richer. Other than that, there was not much difference.

The chill I had on my neck was the warning I get when danger is nearby. I still had that cool feeling.

So it wasn't just Tim Dukes, even though he was somehow connected to it. I knew I would find out real soon what the connection was.

I went inside the jail and pulled out my wanted posters to see if Tim Dukes was on one of them. He wasn't on a wanted poster, but I found the telegram stating Tim had shot and injured a man called Cherokee Bob in Durango, Colorado, a couple of months ago. Since we now had telegraph lines to almost every large city, we received a telegram on every shooting if it was a report on someone the sheriffs and US marshals thought could be trouble for us. Cherokee Bob was on one of the posters and a fifty-dollar reward was out for his capture. Bo Willis would eventually kill Cherokee and collect the bounty. His name was now on the list of gunmen who were thought to be fast guns. He couldn't live up to it!

Someone would try to build his reputation on killing Tim Duke and would be challenged to a duel wherever he went until someone beat- or killed - him. Tim actually had mortally wounded Cherokee Bob when he'd shattered Cherokee's right elbow in a gunfight but it wasn't until a few months later that Cherokee Bob died, when Bo Willis finished him off.

Everyone had expected Tim to be killed when challenged by Cherokee Bob. Tim was soft-spoken and well mannered. Cherokee Bob had been thought of as a fast gun. He also had been arrogant. According to the telegram, he had badgered Tim into the gunfight. Tim had been sitting in a corner at the back of the Buffalo Café drinking coffee when Cherokee Bob had come into the café. It was a quiet day in the café. It only took a few minutes for Cherokee Bob to decide to humiliate Tim.

He strutted over to the table Tim was sitting at. He said, "Get up and give me that chair." He picked up Tim's cup of coffee and drank about half of it. He took Tim's hat off his head and poured the rest of the coffee into it. Tim sat quietly until he had had enough.

He got up slowly, moved back a step, and told Cherokee Bob, "You have two choices: you can buy me another cup of coffee and a new hat or you can back up your bad manners and die.

Cherokee laughed and started to say something when, all at once, he knew he had made a terrible mistake. He didn't have a choice or a chance. He had to fight. He went for his gun. He never got it out. Tim shot Cherokee, shattering his right elbow. He hit what he'd been aiming at. Although the man who killed Cherokee Bob collected on him, Tim really killed Cherokee Bob when he blew his right elbow away. The telegram said Cherokee Bob stayed out of Durango while he practiced drawing his gun with his left hand. He came back in when he thought he was just as fast as ever. He wasn't! The first day he came back to town, he tried it out on an old rangy cowboy named Bo Willis. Bo tried to avoid killing Cherokee Bob, but he had no choice in the matter. Cherokee Bob didn't get his gun out of his holster this time either. On a cold, rainy day in Durango, Colorado, they buried Cherokee Bob in an unmarked grave. After a few months, no one remembered who was buried there.

Tim heard a big man talking about Tom Davis murdering eight men by leaving them in the desert without guns, horses, or food. Tim figured his brother Rodney was one of them. He had been only a few weeks behind Rodney. He'd thought he could change Rodney if he could find him. Rodney had not been well liked by anyone, but it did help them remember him. Tim had moved on to Santa Fe where he'd planned to look me up. I wasn't hard to find since I was the marshal. In Tim's eyes, my title meant nothing. Tim had waited long enough to settle it and wanted to finish it. The big man who had told Tim about his brother and the desert was Ron Jedrokoski. That was where the connection I felt with Tim came from.

Both of us survived the long anticipated duel with only minor injuries. After applying bandages to Tim's wounds, Doc walked his patient to my jail. He must have said something to Tim to change his mind about me because Tim said, "I'm sorry. I should have known better." Doc looked at my wound. He put something on it that burned for a while. He said, "I told you that one day someone like Tim, who is about as fast as you are, will kill you because you try to shoot their gun out of their hand. You need to shoot to kill."

I knew Doc was right. I had grown tired of shooting good cowboys who were letting off some steam.

I told Tim, "Forget it. Would you like to work during the winter on the ranch my friend Cowboy and I own together? You might get some work as a deputy. It's about twenty-five miles west of here." Tim thought about it for a few seconds before he accepted it. I had run a great many gunmen out of Santa Fe, and a lot of merchants were mad at me. They forgot how Santa Fe had been before I'd become town marshal.

After I talked to Tim, I put some of my Apache herbs on my wound. Then I put some on Tim's wounds. Doc wouldn't get his feelings hurt if he didn't know it. Doc didn't believe in Indian medicine. I did. It had always worked on me. Doc went on back to his office. I would send his breakfast over in a few minutes. The herbs took a day to clean the wounds up, but they did the job.

Tim believed me now because of what Doc had told him and the fact that I hadn't killed him when I could have. My sixth sense told me I would need some good gun hands like Tim as friends since trouble was coming soon.

Cowboy and I owned a ranch together. We bought and raised nearly 2,000 steers from poor ranchers who had faced a drought the past two years. It was always a battle between cattle and location. We could ship them back east by rail now. The railroads had tracks all across the whole country.

We were lucky our ranch had a deep spring that had never run dry. We paid top dollar for the steers and had told them we would buy more of them if they had them.

CHAPTER 3

Cowboy

Cowboy's real name was Billy Sunday. Ira Goodnight (son of Charles Goodnight), Cowboy, and I had become partners in Tucson, Arizona, after they'd seen me beat Ron Jedrokoski to a pulp even though he was much bigger than I was. Ron was an evil bully.

Cowboy, Ira, and I had driven a herd of cows to Abilene, Kansas, along with big John Chisum. We'd sold them for top dollar. Ira had been killed. We each had a large amount of money in the Bank of Abilene. We'd sent Ira's share to his father, who was famous for breaking new trails to get his cattle to new marketplaces so he could get a better price for them.

Cowboy and I had been talking about a name for the ranch we owned between us. I'd kidded Cowboy, saying, "We ought to name the ranch 'Rosita's Place.' Then you can remember how close you come to having a grave in Mexico."

Rosita was the sheriff's girlfriend down in Del Rios, Mexico. She liked Cowboy and had told him so since the sheriff had been out of town. The sheriff had come back unexpectedly, and Cowboy had beaten the sheriff to the border by only a few minutes. I quit teasing him because I thought he was going to have a nervous breakdown. We named the spread the Longest

Drive. When Cowboy married Beth in May, I would give my part of the ranch to them.

I received a telegram telling me some Comanche warriors had jumped the Fort Stanton Reservation. I didn't get much information on the breakout. I rode out to notify my father, Brother Nate, Cowboy, and Don Luis Montoya that the Comanche were on the warpath. The telegrams almost always meant trouble. This time was no exception.

It did give me a chance to visit briefly with my family and friends. Everything was fine with them. Wedding preparations were going on even though the wedding of Beth to Cowboy was still over seven months from now. My mother, Jane, didn't think they had enough time left. Dad didn't make any comments one way or the other. He was proving again that he was a wise man.

Cowboy sent one of his vaqueros over to tell Don Luis Montoya of the Comanche breakout. Don Luis notified everyone else. I told my father about the Comanche. He was like he always was. He could handle it. Don Luis would send five of his men to stay with my family until the Comanche came back in. It was good to see them again. Dad, Mom, and Beth didn't get to come to Santa Fe very often except now with the wedding preparations going on. Mom had to get Beth the perfect dresses since this was going to be an old Southern wedding, dance cotillion and all. Beth would have to have at least four flowing dresses to wear during the two-day celebration. Don Luis had graciously let the marriage take place at his ranch, the only ranch big enough to have the wedding.

Cowboy almost missed the wedding. He was out scattering the steers so the Comanche would not find them all in one place. The Comanche could not afford to spend a lot of time searching for them.

Cowboy didn't know what warned him, but something did. He jerked his horse around and saw several men behind him. He raced for the narrow arroyo a couple of miles in front of him. He was riding Jubilee, his fastest horse. Jubilee flew. Cowboy could see another group of men racing down the right side of the arroyo. They had a slight edge on him. The exit to the arroyo was only a few hundred yards from him. So were the ones on the right bank. He didn't have time to wonder why the men were chasing him. As they closed the distance, they began shooting. A bullet stung Jubilee on the rump. Jubilee, hid briefly by some boulders forming a slight curve, jumped sideways, throwing Cowboy off. He hit the ground hard, knocking him unconscious.

Jubilee climbed up the low bank without being seen. He never broke stride running back to Cowboy's ranch.

Cowboy, now barely conscious, noticed a small hole in the boulders on the bottom of the arroyo. He was about to go under. He knew the outlaws would kill him if he did not hide. He climbed into the hole and over a ledge inside the cave before becoming totally unconscious.

A small trail of blood led into the cave. Stefano, their best tracker, saw the place where Jubilee had left the arroyo. He thought Cowboy had gotten away even though he believed he had hit Cowboy at least once. Stefano noticed the difference in the depths of the hoof prints of Jubilee coming out of the arroyo. They were not quite as deep as the ones in the arroyo. All the others had ridden on when he decided to back track Cowboy a short distance. He was about to turn around and join the others when he saw the small trail of blood. He could tell Cowboy had barely been able to crawl into the cave. What he didn't know was that some rattlesnakes had denned up for the winter in the cave. They were sluggish but not dormant. Cowboy had fallen into the only vacant spot in the cave. The rattlers had shaken their tales a little when Cowboy had fallen into the cave, but they had settled down since he lay unconscious, not moving. Stefano smiled when he saw the blood. He was going to make the hundred dollars put on Cowboy's head by the marshal of Phoenix. Stefano shot once into the air. The other men got to him just as he crawled into the cave. He couldn't see very well, so he extended his hand. He touched the rough side of a giant rattler who had heard the shot and become alarmed. Stefano's blood ran ice cold as he jerked his hand away from the snake. The giant rattler followed the arm and struck just above it.

Stefano screamed and jerked, trying to get out of the cave and away from the rattler. The fangs of the snake hit Stefano in his left eye, one fang in the eye and the other one penetrating the thin bone on the side of the eye. The rattler hung on as Stefano flopped out of the cave screaming.

Watson heard Stefano screaming, "Shoot him!" So he did. He shot Stefano in his face, killing him and the snake at the same time. Stefano would not have lived anyway.

No one thought that Cowboy could be in the cave, and even if they had, they would not crawl into it. The giant rattlers were about the only thing that scared some of the men. Cowboy still lay unconscious in the cave. Since he didn't move, the snakes finally settled down. All the outlaws could think of was getting back to a saloon and getting a glass of cold beer. They fussed about what a bad day they'd had. They didn't know it was going to get worse—much worse.

Cowboy's horse galloped up to the corral at Cowboy's ranch.

Ramon, the foreman for Don Luis Montoya, had come over with two of his men to help Cowboy scatter the cattle to a safer place. He knew immediately that Cowboy was in trouble.

He didn't say a word. He grabbed his horse and took off, following Jubilee's tracks. He figured Cowboy was a few miles away since his horse was covered with sweat. It was pouring off him. They came to the part of the canyon where Jubilee had climbed the bank. They saw the body of Stefano with the snake still attached to him.

Ramon said, "The coyotes will eat well tonight." Ramon saw right away what had happened. He told the men with him, "Cowboy has to be in the cave with snakes all around him. There are no signs of him leaving the cave." Ramon got the men working; making torches out of dry mesquite bushes that would burn hot with heavy smoke coming from them. They made several torches. Ramon made a mask that covered his nose and mouth. He took one of the torches, lit it, and stuck the flaming torch slowly into the cave. The rattlers had been disturbed twice, and they were really agitated now. You could hear some of the snakes dropping off the ledges, trying to get away from the heavy smoke. They had their rattlers shaking a mile a minute. Ramon lit another torch. He dropped the first torch close to Cowboy. He cautiously looked around. He saw several rattlers slithering away, going deeper into the cave. He saw Cowboy lying on the floor with a large snake coiled up on his chest. The snake was using Cowboy's body heat to keep warm since they had no way for their bodies to generate heat or coolness. Ramon lit another torch and dropped the burning torch he used to light the first. The snake slid back a little with his tail warning Ramon that it was getting mad. The snakes, all but the one on Cowboy, moved further back. Ramon slid slowly into the cave, always holding the torch between him and the snake. It looked like the snake was going to hold his ground until the fire and the smoke finally made him retreat. It was lucky for Ramon and Cowboy that the cave ran pretty deep so the snakes were not forced by the smoke to come out of the front of the cave. The smoke was almost choking Ramon even though he had tied a kerchief over his nose and mouth. It helped some.

Gervis could not get inside the cave to help pull Cowboy out until Ramon crawled in beside Cowboy. He rolled him over and put him on Ramon's back. Ramon slowly lifted Cowboy up. He crawled up to the opening. Only a strong man could have done it in the narrow space. Ramon got him to the opening where Gervis could help pull Cowboy out. With Ramon lifting and Gervis pulling, they began to slide him out of the cave. He was still unconscious. It took several more minutes and tries before Gervis and Ramon finally got him out of the cave. They examined him. He had lost a little blood, but the wound was not serious. The knot on his head could be serious. They made a travois to carry Cowboy back to his ranch.

Ramon sent two men back to the ranch with Cowboy after they made pressure bandages to stop the bleeding. Ramon would go into town and send Doc out to look at Cowboy. Ramon had treated enough bullet wounds to know when they were life threatening. He had seen a few concussions also. The trail to town was also the trail the outlaws were taking. Ramon would check on that also. It was a broad trail that led to the Palace Saloon.

He entered town and went straight to Doc's office. Doc was pulling a tooth since he was also the dentist. He gave the cowpuncher a big swallow of whiskey. He motioned to Ramon to hold the cowpuncher down as he yanked the tooth out. Ramon had no problem holding the man down after the shot of cocaine put the cowpuncher to sleep. Ramon had other business in town he had to get to. I had just released a rustler, and I'd told Ramon about him. Ramon said, "Cocaine is a good way to handle a bad prisoner. It helps get him into a cell quietly." The prisoner had been discovered killing a cow. It had been his second one. Since he didn't have a family to feed, the second steer made him a rustler. Jim Taylor, the owner of the cows, had ridden up on the rustler, who had offered to share a cow with him. He was taking the rest of the cows to a nester family that was out of food. I had gotten to them at about the same time. Jim had had three choices. He could hang him, let the hanging judge have him, or let him go with the meat. Jim had told me to give the rustler a lecture and the two cows. I had. Jim had helped the rustler cut and carry the meat to the needy family. Jim had told the rustler he could not tell them that he was the one giving it to them. Jim had told the rustler, "Next time, you come to me." One day, the nester would have to move anyway.

Ramon noticed the nine horses tied to the hitching rail of the Palace. He came to the jail and told me about Cowboy's ambush and wound. My deputy, Andrew, wanted to go with us over to the Palace. It made the odds nine to three. The odds were just about right. Maybe they were slightly in our favor.

We walked over to the Palace Saloon. Ramon and I went in the front door. Andrew went in the back door. The place was empty except for the nine men and the bartender, who was glad to see us. It was my play to start the action since Cowboy was my partner and friend. I was looking forward to this.

Bill Parham, the leader of the outlaws said, "We don't drink with greasers or marshals."

Ramon told the bartender, "I will have tequila, and then my friend, the marshal here, will have a discussion with these bad men."

I said over my shoulder to Ramon, "I will take the loudmouth and the two dogs next to him. You take the three men on the right side, and Andrew can clean up the last three. If you run out of targets, shoot any of them who are still standing or these cowards can take off their guns and boots and stand in the corner." Four of them complied. They had decided they wanted to live.

Bill Parham was stunned. He watched Ramon sip his last swallow of tequila and his four men standing in the corner. One of them was Pasqual, and he was no coward. Ramon's, Andrew's, and my eyes had gone cold and deadly. Bill hadn't started anything yet because he had a bad feeling. All his men were watching him, waiting for the signal. As Ramon set his empty glass down, Bill

Parham nodded his head and went for his gun. I killed him before he stopped nodding. I shot the man on Bill's right before he could turn his head to follow the action. He shook his head, wet his pants as he threw his gun on the floor, and fell down. One of Andrew's targets stepped behind a post, went out the other side, and stepped right into a bullet from Andrew. Andrew wounded him. He could have killed the man if he had wanted to. Ramon just pulled the trigger, and one was knocked backward, dropping his adversary dead on the spot.

Ramon told Andrew, "Showing mercy to those who don't deserve it will get you killed." When the smoke cleared away, there were two dead, three wounded, and four live cowards. I sent the cowards on a long, barefoot walk to Albuquerque and then on out of the territory with a promise that I would kill any of them who came back. I let them have two guns between them, each one loaded with one bullet. They left in a hurry without their boots. The three wounded men were taken over to Doc's office. Doc had left thirty minutes ago to see about Cowboy. Since Doc wouldn't be back for at least a day, the wounded men would probably be in for a bad time. One might not make it. Good riddance! Jessie Taylor knew something about bullet wounds, so I sent for him to come and look at the wounded men. The coward didn't know anything except someone said there was one hundred dollars for Cowboy's scalp.

I suggested he go east where being a man wouldn't have to be as tough. He left that night.

I knew the big game with Ron had just started for me. It was the same for Don Luis Montoya, Dad, Nate, Cowboy, and others. Whoever was behind this, and I believed it was Ron Jedrokoski, now had the worst enemies he could have. He didn't know it, but he soon would.

I gained two friends. Tim Dukes became our foreman at our ranch, and the bartender, Joe Miles, became our friend and listening post. The bartender had his scattergun ready just in case we needed him. I knew who my enemy was for sure now. It was Ron Jedrokoski. He would never forget the beating I'd given him and how we had broken up his crooked games at the army base at Tucson, Arizona.

CHAPTER 4

The Comanche

The Comanche had nothing to lose. It was their last hurrah. Unless I changed things, the warriors would be killed or moved to Florida.

A telegram came to me saying, "Sauktauk has been killed by drunken soldiers." I knew they were probably some soldiers acting drunk. Sauktauk was my blood brother. If the Comanche had not taken care of the killers of Sauktauk and his wife, I would have. The soldiers had been trying to force Sauktauk's wife to go with them. No one had ever challenged Sauktauk before. The soldiers had always walked carefully around him. He'd known they must have decided to go on and kill him. He had tried to avoid trouble, but he'd known they would eventually kill him. He had been ready to go to the other world.

In his heart and mind, three words described him—"he was ready." He held himself in check as long as he could even though he had terrible angry spells. He was mostly mad at himself. He had led them to this. A lot of them had already lost their pride and honor. He had believed the white eyes again. He would never learn his lesson, it seemed.

Life on the reservations was bad. They treated the Indians like they were children. Even most of the chiefs were treated that way.

Some members of his tribe did act like children. The people on the reservation traded them raw moonshine that had stuff in it that could make you go blind and crazy. For some reason, most Indians couldn't hold their whiskey. Some of the warriors would sell a night with their wives to the soldiers for a bottle of this poison. When the whiskey was gone and they began to sober up, they got mad at themselves. Since they could do nothing to the soldiers, they beat up their wives. Some had gambled away their belongings, even their horses, just to get a bottle of the raw whiskey.

Sauktauk wouldn't let the soldier have Saguita. He knew this was a way to make him fight. He was already fighting a losing fight against the Indian agent and the soldiers. He would rather die than live without honor. He would never let them treat him as a child, not as a man. He would never shame his wife. He knew they were baiting him so they could kill him. He knew he would not survive this encounter and neither would Saguita. There were too many soldiers around them. It was a good day to die. He drew his knife. He was so quick, the soldier talking to him never realized his throat had been cut until the blood spurted out. Sauktauk spun around and stabbed another soldier. Several of the soldiers shot him. Another soldier shot Saguita, who also had her knife in her hand. It killed her instantly. Sauktauk got one more soldier before they killed him. The soldiers were never held responsible for the outbreak. The Comanche were blamed for all of it. It didn't matter to the Comanche who got the blame. They were on their last hurrah. The Comanche felt betrayed. They jumped the reservation. They were determined to avenge Sauktauk. They killed four soldiers, two civilians, and the Indian agent. All of them had treated the Comanche badly in the past. They took all the food as well as all the rifles and ammunition they could carry.

They got warm clothing from the supply office. Winter was about to roar out of the Rockies, due north of them.

They didn't harm anyone else or destroy any government property. Since the soldiers were only a small detail occupying the barracks and since the Comanche were so strong with anger, the remaining soldiers sat quietly. The Comanche would have the last word. The soldiers who had killed Sauktauk and Saguita were killed in a special way.

They were tied to a pole. Each woman had a sharp skinning knife. The Comanche women always carried the knives with them even though very little skinning was done. They walked around the soldiers tied to the pole and stuck the points of their knives into them. It cut a small line all around the soldiers. The cut was not deep enough to kill, but the loss of blood was. One of the soldiers lived for several hours before dying. The Comanche honored him by not mutilating him like they did the others.

The Indian agent had a special treat for him. He had to run the gauntlet with Comanche women on each side of the line. They let him run a couple of times, with the women trying to break his arms with their heavy clubs. They inflicted many hits on him. However, if he could run it one more time, the Comanche, by their own laws, would let him go.

Just about the time he thought he was going to make it, they brought out the clubs with nails in them. He was lucky one of the women slipped as she swung at him and her club hit his neck. He bled to death very quickly.

The Comanche got the civilians and the soldiers who had no part in killing Sauktauk together and took them several miles from the fort and then let them go, telling them, "You are not to return to the fort until tomorrow at noon." The captives, who had expected to be killed, almost collapsed in relief. They had expected to be tortured also. It gave the Comanche time to get away. When a small platoon of soldiers who had been out on maneuvers came back in the next day, they found a deserted fort and the telegram line cut. They found a spotless camp. Only an hour had passed when they heard the commotion of the soldiers and civilians coming back to the fort. Although they had feared the worst, when rounded up and taken out of the fort, they had not been harmed. Only the ones involved in the killing of Sauktauk and his wife had been killed. The inhabitants of the fort had been given water. No bodies were found. They never suspected the bodies were buried not far away from the reservation. The soldiers and civilians who were not bothered spoke up for the Comanche. Fifty-two warriors had left the reservation knowing they were going to get killed sooner or later. They had chosen to die rather than live the terrible life they were living. It was a good time to die.

Visions

I remembered one of my worst visions. It was the death of Victorio, Morning Star, and one hundred of his Apache. They had been dead about four years. He and his Apaches had left the Fort Apache Reservation and fought the United States and Mexico for over a year. They had eventually been killed on top of a peak on Tres Castille Mountains, Three Castles Mountains, of Candelabra located in Mexico.

An old Mexican Indian fighter had had about three hundred men with him. Each of them had lost someone to the Apache. They'd had an unlimited amount of bullets, guns, and supplies.

Victorio, the shaman, and I had had visions in the past of this happening to Victorio. He had gotten tired of running, or he didn't think the Mexican Indian hunters could slip up on him. Nana was off hunting for food, so he survived. Chato was killed trying to help some women down the peak they were on. The women and children who survived were taken back to Mexico as slaves. They were taught to be domestic servants.

Victorio was down to his last two bullets and one arrow. The Mexicans began their final approach. The Apache were behind rocks, so the Mexicans just shot into the rocks around them until a ricocheting bullet hit the Apache hiding behind them. Victorio curled his body over Morning Star to protect her. Morning Star reached out to touch Victorio. A ricochet hit her in the chest.

She died instantly with her hand lying on Victorio's shoulder. The three hundred Mexicans surrounding Victorio and his warriors fired bullet after bullet into the rocks around them. He saw one Mexican crossing an open place and used his last arrow. He had two bullets left. He saw a foot extending out from a boulder. He shot it. When the Mexican sat up, Victorio shot him.

Victorio pulled his knife out and started down the peak to attack the nearest Mexicans. He was so engrossed in the battle that he didn't feel the slap of the bullet when it hit him. It turned him slightly when another bullet hit him in the head, killing him instantly. When the battle was over and the story hit the papers, it was amazing how many Mexicans claimed to have killed Victorio. A rumor started that he had killed himself. Everyone who knew him knew better.

This had occurred just about the time I had the gunfight with Black Jack Ketchem. Susan had killed Larry Stallings, one of Ketchem's men, just as he'd been about to ambush me. Cowboy had killed another gunman who'd been located in the second-story window of a building. Cowboy had gotten there just in time. The man had raised his rifle to shoot me when Cowboy had turned loose with both barrels of his shotgun. The dust had flown when the gunman had landed spread-eagled down in the street. The shotgun had blown him through the window.

I had planned to go home and work with Dad on his ranch. I'd met Susan, and all my plans to spend just a few days in Santa Fe, New Mexico had been forgotten. After I had proven myself, they'd asked me to be town marshal. I'd checked on my family, found them well and safe, and accepted the job. Two men had offered me the job as marshal of Santa Fe. One of them was Jake. He owned the livery stables. The other one was McGregor, who owned the mercantile store and almost everything else in Santa

Fe. They'd had a lot of problems since Bert Goodall, the last marshal, had been killed. No one else wanted the job. They really were glad I took it. I accepted the badge and knew that it marked me as a target. Marshals were not very popular with cowboys, who had been punching steers thirty or forty days without any of the nicer things in life. I preferred talking to them if I could. Some wouldn't talk to me at all. They were only dangerous if they had a few friends with them. Every so often, a mean gunman came into town, got drunk, and went crazy. After I hit a few over the head and killed one man who had shot my deputy, everything slowed down. It hadn't taken long to clean up Santa Fe.

After a couple of years, Santa Fe was a quiet town. It was too quiet for some of the merchants in town. Ranchers, like my dad and Don Luis, could and did handle their own problems. The towns had to handle their own problems.

McGregor was the unofficial mayor of Santa Fe. He was also smart to hire me as the town's marshal.

CHAPTER 6

Johnny Comanche

I was about halfway to my father's ranch to warn him of the Comanche when I saw a slight movement high up on the ridge to my left. A hawk flew out of a bush. This alone did not alarm me. My sixth sense kicking in did. I saw a Comanche warrior sitting his horse up among the boulders. He was the reason the hawk took flight. In this land, knowing what caused the flight was really what gave you a chance to survive. I automatically got ready for an ambush even though I knew that it had to be a very young, inexperienced warrior since he was half in the sunshine and half in the shade. If he were an Apache boy, he would be sent back to the ten-year-old boys in training.

I decided to teach him a lesson in this game of warfare we were playing. The Apache and Comanche looked at battles or fights between them as games they loved to play. Counting coup (touching your enemy with your bare hand instead of hitting him with your tomahawk) was treated with the utmost respect since it was so dangerous. On occasion, the Apache and the Comanche would have a battle with each side trying to kill the other side. A couple of days after that, they might have a stick ball game between the two tribes. They would have horse races. The losers forfeited their horses. The most dangerous game was the wrestling matches. Broken bones were common. The best athlete of all the tribes was a member of the Sac and Fox tribe with the name Jim Thorpe. White Killer had been the most formidable one in Victorio's tribe.

It had to be a single warrior. There was only one place suitable for an ambush, and it was further on. I was closer to it than he was. I waited until I got past the Comanche before I nudged Sugar Foot along. I got there only a couple of minutes before he did. He rode up and got off his horse. Something made him look over his shoulder. I was sitting on a small boulder with my rifle held loosely on him. He almost made a mistake and tried to take me. He was totally surprised. I talked to him in sign language.

"Why do you wish to kill me? I have no quarrel with you. I am blood brother to Sauktauk, great chief of the Comanche. I am Lone Eagle, the White Apache."

The young warrior blanched. He had heard many stories around the nightly campfires of Lone Eagle and his exploits.

The story of how Lone Eagle and ten of his warriors killed seventy-four Comanche after their raid on Victorio's village had been told to him many times. Comanche was also familiar with the knife fight I'd had with Sauktauk. I could have killed Sauktauk, but I'd let him go. The stories told to Comanche about Lone Eagle would live as long as there were Comanche Indians.

He repeated the story of Sauktauk's death told to me by others. He said, "Sauktauk is dead, killed by drunken soldiers. Saguita, his wife, is dead also. It is as it always has been. The White Eyes cannot be trusted. Their words are like grains of sand blowing in the wind. The sand does not control where its destiny is. It goes where the wind wills it to go. We Comanche have always been free. Now we are like the sand."

"What are you called? How old are you?"

"I am called Johnny Comanche, and I am fourteen winters old. I have not received my name from Ussen, but I am prepared for it. I will die with my head held high, and I will be remembered. I will seek out the enemies of the Comanche and kill some of them before they get me. That is why I was going to kill you. What would you do in my place? I have no reason to live."

I corrected him, saying, "You have every reason to live! Your people need you to help them through this bad time. All of you must learn the good ways of the White-Eye life and continue on with the good ways of the Comanche. Don't do the evil things that will take away your honor or the honor of the Comanche. Your people do need you to lead them where they will have to go. I have had a vision about you. It is good, and it will come true. I will help you find the path that will lead you to your destiny if you wish me to do so."

The young, soon-to-be warrior realized he had been thinking only of himself. Tom wrote a message to Cowboy.

Tom told Johnny, "Go to my ranch and give Cowboy this note. He will gladly hire you. We will work this out." You can work on our ranch until I get back. Then you and I will go to your reservation. Be sure you have a white flag attached to your bow. Someone will see you right away at our ranch. This note will keep you safe." It was a good deal for both of us.

The note read, "One day, Johnny is going to be important to us and the Indian reservations. Ussen told me in a vision how Johnny had a hawk fly into their camp when Johnny was born. He perched on the top of the teepee Johnny and his mother were in. Ussen has his name ready to give to him. He has not earned it yet. He will change his name to Johnny Hawk Comanche in the future. Johnny Comanche is an honorable name. He will earn the name Johnny Hawk Comanche. It will be his." He was about to earn it. That night, Johnny had a vision. So did I. Although he'd had the name "Johnny Hawk" picked out for him, he could not be called Johnny Hawk until he got older and did something spectacular to earn it.

In my dream, I saw a golden hawk riding the thermals high in the sky. He slid from one updraft of heated air to another, flying without any visible effort. With his keen eyesight, he could see a flock of five crows flying way down below him. The crows knew he was up there. As long as they stayed below thirty feet, they were safe. If the hawk dove at them while they were at least that low, he would crash into the ground.

The hawk automatically figured how high the crows were. One crow was braver than the others. He gradually increased the height he was flying until he reached forty feet. He could spill the air from under his wings and lose altitude in a hurry if he had to. He figured he was safe at forty feet.

The hawk had him timed. He flapped his wings, pulled his feathers tighter, and folded his body up to streamline it. He struck the crow, burying his talons deep into the body of the crow. A loud squawking arose from the other crows. The hawk pulled out of the dive, barely making it, and flew slowly and awkwardly toward their nest where the young hawks were.

Three young hawks were spending their last day in it. It was time for them to go out on their own. The cycles of living and dying would continue.

The crows sensed an easy kill since the golden hawk was overloaded and close to the ground. All they had to do was force the hawk to land, and the five remaining crows could overwhelm him. They would peck him to death.

High above them with the sun at her back, the female hawk saw the crows about to catch her mate. She hit the four crows like a thunderbolt, killing one of them and knocking two others out of the sky. The two crows that were not killed or wounded flew off in different directions. They'd had enough.

The three young hawks were ready to join the battle for survival. At least the mother hawk was ready for them to fly away. It was time for another cycle of life to begin for her. The runt of the hawks in the nest was smaller because he was not big enough to compete with his bigger brother and sister for the food brought to them by their father and mother. It started earlier that morning. The runt was driven over to the edge of the nest and then forced on over it. He was smaller, but he was strong since he had to fight every day to live. He tumbled into space, just missing the edge of the canyon below him. He spread his wings and brought himself into the position to fly. He was panicked when he went over the side of the nest, so he flapped his wings as hard as he could. To his amazement, he began to climb. He caught a thermal and soared upward. He spilled some air from his wings, gradually dropping slowly until he flew into another thermal. He flew in and out of the heated air. He was the master of the sky as he learned to dive. He found he could slow his dive down by spreading his wings.

In a short period of time, he could control most of the things necessary for him to be able to survive flying. He had something he had to finish. The two larger hawks were in the nest waiting for the last meal provided by their parents. The runt got several hundred feet above the nest. He flew almost straight down and struck the two hawks.

One of the two hawks struck by the runt fell out of the nest. Since his left wing was now broken, he could not fly. He bounced off the side of the canyon several times, landing in a pile of loose feathers. If he were not already dead, a predator would get him. His sister was knocked over to the side of the nest, herself slightly injured. The father got there with the dead crow about that time. He used his sharp beak to tear the crow open and pull strips of meat that he fed to the young hawks. The strongest hawk was always fed the most. This time was the first and only time the runt got his fill before the bigger sister started eating. The mother hawk got back about then, and after the biggest young female hawk finished feeding, she pushed her over the edge. It was time for her to fly or die. She flew. The runt finished his meal and took off flying south. So did his sister. At the end of the canyon, they separated, going their different ways south. Neither of them looked back at the nest or at their parents. The cycle of life continued for the hawks. I woke up, knowing I had seen Johnny Comanche's future. He was the runt.

He would be tested, and he would win many battles for the Indians as a senator from New Mexico.

I warned Dad, Nate, and Cowboy. Nate sent a message to Don Luis to send riders to every ranch within a fifty-mile radius.

The warning made Nate change his usual order of doing things on his ranch.

CHAPTER 7

The Killer, El Diablo

It was the beginning of an all-out war between Ron Jedrokoski and me, although I didn't know it at the time. Ron had made himself marshal of Phoenix.

A wanted poster had been put out for me with a $1,000 reward- dead or alive. Plans had been made and men were assigned to carry them out. One such killer was El Diablo, the Devil. Nate, my brother, was his target. El Diablo was like an artist. He left his signature on every person he killed. He was a one-shot artist. He had never missed yet. My father and mother, brother, sister, Cowboy, and his wife were each worth one hundred dollars dead. Ron was putting up the money

A gang of outlaws worked for Ron, who had found a new way to get rich. He forced the business owners to play poker with him. He didn't show his cards. He just told them what he had. He now owned six saloons and a whole lot of the red-light district. He also owned a couple of regular businesses. After crippling one of the property owners and beating the other up pretty badly, he had his way. Phoenix had several gold and silver mines that were productive. Ron left them alone since he would wind up with the money and the mines anyway, just like he got his saloons and red-light property. It also made a difference that there were several German miners who were as big and strong as he was.

Ron had waited as long as he could. He wanted all my family and friends dead. He had the money to pay for it. Gunmen had been sent to ambush Cowboy and Nate since they were isolated. Cowboy got a concussion that lasted about a week. He was ready to get even. He should have been easy to kill. He wasn't. Ron lost ten men trying to ambush Cowboy.

Ron wanted me for his own kill.

Nate had one of the kind killers looking for him. He was a lot more expensive than the other killers, but Ron thought he was worth it.

The man with the rifle laid motionless up on the hillside above Nate's casa. He was a perfect killing machine. He had no qualms about shooting anyone, including women and children. He had no emotions. He never wondered how he could kill in cold blood and did not feel any remorse about the killing. He moved into his position on the ridge a few minutes before dawn. He had his scope ready to be attached to his rifle. His tripod was set up to keep the rifle steady. He could shoot without the tripod, but the kill was more certain with it. He had been by Nate's house a couple of weeks ago and had picked out his place to shoot from. He knew the layout of the ranch and the best place to shoot from. He attached the scope.

He was so good at his job of killing that his presence didn't disturb the wildlife too much. They recognized that he was the top predator and that he was not interested in them. He had a better target. El Diablo always shot only one bullet and quickly left the scene. He was not interested in fame, money, or friendship. He was a loner who did not mind it. The only love in his life was his rifle. He loved the shooting. The harder the shot, the better he liked it.

A pair of fighting scorpions stopped their fight and went their separate ways when El Diablo lay down beside them. Being paid $250 for the killing of Nate would help enhance his reputation. He was a big threat as a predator. A coyote passing through turned and went back the way he had come.

Not many men had ever heard of El Diablo. To tell the truth, almost all of them who had heard of him had never met him or seen him. He let a third party arrange the business part of the shooting. Everyone involved was terribly afraid of him and had no wish to meet him. Senator Vallee, one of the people with power, had decided to pay only half the fee agreed upon. Two days later, El Diablo had made a marvelous shot, wounding Buzz Vallee, who had been standing between two men. Buzz had fallen, knocking over the podium. El Diablo had smiled. Buzz Vallee would never run for public office again or beat him out of his money. The shot had been made at three hundred yards. It had hit Buzz in the chest. El Diablo had smiled again. Being a senator hadn't saved Buzz from being shot. El Diablo thought he was invincible; it had been an easy shot. He'd leaked the news that El Diablo had enforced his laws. Senator Vallee had paid the rest of the money he owed to El Diablo and resigned from the senate. El Diablo made everyone who came in contact with him feel creepy just like him, even though they had no idea that he was El Diablo. He gave off an aura of total evil. He didn't know it and wouldn't care if he did.

Ramon and I were not afraid of him. We were planning on meeting El Diablo very soon. Don Luis had lost one man to El Diablo. They had found him propped up against a tree with a sign on him that read, "325 yards." El Diablo had left his marker on him. It had been just a practice shot for the Devil.

A rumor had come up from one of the saloons, and then another one repeated the rumor: Nate was as good as dead. One of his vaqueros, just back from Santa Fe also had heard it in a saloon where most of his Spanish friends drank. The rumor was that someone who never missed was after Nate. The only way they could be sure that it was more than a rumor was for someone to stay at Nate's ranch to help him guard the place. They had to get the shooter first. They couldn't give him a clean shot because he never missed. The only name that good Ramon had heard of was a shooter called El Diablo. No one knew or paid any attention to El Diablo. No one could describe him. He did nothing to call their attention to him. They looked right through him. It had been that way since he was born. His father had not been one who hugged or touched anyone. His mother had been forced to lead the same kind of life. She had felt unloved also. There had been no Christmas, Thanksgiving, or any celebration ever in his father's house. He'd been sixteen when the break he'd been waiting for had come.

He found a single-shot rifle lying beside a man that had too much whiskey to drink. He took the rifle, bullets, and what little money the drunk had on him. He shot the man and left town. He had not ever regretted his decision to leave. One day, he would go back and kill his father. Two days later and twenty-one miles down the road, he came to Allenburg, Pennsylvania. It was a small town that was having a turkey shoot. To his surprise, he entered it and won the turkey. The point of the turkey shoot was to shoot at only the head of the turkey. He was the third contestant. The turkey was in a box with only his head showing. It was only a two-hundred-yard shot. He was the only one who made it. One of the men he beat wanted to have a contest between him and Joeb (as he was known then.) Joeb shot the heads off two more turkeys at 250 yards. The crowd started betting against him at 275 yards. Everyone quit betting against him after three hundred yards. Everyone remembered the great shooting and no one remembered what the shooter looked like. He wound up with a horse, a pistol, and thirty-two dollars. A couple of men looking on the contest planned to take the winnings from him when he left the area. They changed their minds after they looked into his deadly yellow eyes. A shiver ran through the two men. They wanted no part of Joeb even though he was only sixteen. He traveled west, exercising his talent along the way. It got to be easier and easier for him to kill animals, not for food, but just to kill them, until finally something happened that was inevitable.

One day, a lone cowboy attracted by the fire of El Diablo asked if he could spend the night at his campfire. Just before dawn, he got up and put the halter on El Diablo's horse. He got his own horse and quietly led the two horses out of the camp.

El Diablo heard the cowboy get up and start leading the horses out. He could simply have killed the cowboy right then, but he wanted to see how far he could shoot accurately. He could see the cowboy clearly since a bright moon lit up the sky. He could have shot the cowboy as soon as he wanted to. He waited until the horse thief thought he was safe. About 350 yards from his camp, the cowboy turned around to look back at the camp. Joeb shot at him. The bullet knocked him out of his saddle. Joeb Taylor signed the note El Diablo and the 350 yardage. From then on, he was "the Devil" and called El Diablo. He changed his name, but no one knew it. Everyone knew about El Diablo later on. No one knew Joeb was El Diablo. He was given credit for every unsolved killing within a five-hundred-mile radius. One day, he was given credit for killings two men on opposite sides of the circle at the same time.

He was called El Diablo from then on, although no one knew him personally. He heard the rumors about himself, but he didn't care either way. He heard his nickname mentioned in saloons all over the west. It sounded good to him. He continued to make his way west, arriving a few weeks later in Cheyenne, Wyoming. By this time, he had mastered his single-shot rifle, the old Henry repeater, and his pistol. When taking aim, he just let himself relax and looked his bullets into his targets. He could cock and shoot his rifles as fast as almost every fast gun could draw and shoot his pistol. Since he had a repeater and a one-shot rifle he used occasionally, he couldn't afford to miss. He didn't. He also had one advantage: The men didn't know about him. Rumors started about the man and his rifle. He was a short, heavyset man dressed in slightly soiled black clothes.

John Cassity was the best gunsmith in the West. He never shared his knowledge of people and their guns with anyone. El Diablo knew what he wanted, and John Cassity knew how to make it. El Diablo wound up with a one-of-a-kind rifle that was accurate up to about five hundred yards. Buffalo guns would shoot that far, but the bullet tumbled. John Cassity had made the special bullets spin by rifling the barrel. The idea of adding a telescope to the specially made .44-caliber rifle had been John's, although both sides in the Civil War had had snipers. Some had had telescopes that were not too good.

El Diablo set up his rifle on a tripod. The gun was ready. He put the crosshairs on the scope on the middle of the door. The rifle was set up for the shot. He would shoot Nate as he came out of the door.

The rifle barrel had been reinforced. John Cassity had fixed it so he could use more gunpowder. El Diablo used a lot more powder in the shells. The rifle weighed fourteen pounds, about four pounds more than the regular repeating rifle. A sling was added to take the weight off his hands and onto his shoulders. The rifle had a special attachment—a metal bar that had holes drilled for brackets to hold the telescopic sight. The telescopic sight was an old naval brass telescope, the best made. It made longer shots possible. Cassity made his own bullets. It made the bullet go further and straighter. Even with the excessive weight, the Devil could shoot his rifle as fast as most gunmen could shoot their pistols. He had surprised a few gunmen already. It's not unusual for gunmen to get in a fast draw contest in front of a crowd and not use bullets. Some gunmen are still like kids. They all remembered his speed, but no one remembered him.

He was ready for the $250 shot offered to him to kill Nate. He'd received a note with Nate's name and location on it a week ago. He always picked his own time to make the one shot. He'd picked up the note in a saloon. He'd slept well that night. He had learned to sleep like the Apache did. He always slept close to his target. The morning air was pure and clean. The cool air was a little bit uncomfortable, but he warmed up as he began to get the rush he always got from a shooting. More time passed until it was time for him to finish this business.

CHAPTER 8

El Diablo's Last Shot

El Diablo was all business now. The telescopic sight was perfectly aligned. The crosshairs split the center of the door. He could sense someone behind the door. It didn't matter if it was Nate or his wife. He would get $100 for her and $250 for him. A quick smile passed across his face. It was one of the few times he smiled. He took a deep breath and put his finger on the trigger. The door moved an inch or so before it stuck. A second pull on the door freed it, and the door slid open. A figure was silhouetted in the middle of the door. The next part of the shooting was where everything came together for him.

El Diablo pulled the trigger, slowly letting out his breath at the same speed. The rifle jerked a little as the figure framed by the door was knocked backward into the room,

El Diablo didn't even look toward his target. After all, he had never missed. He took the scope off of the rifle, dismantled the rifle, and put it all in the special case he had made for it. He was at least one hundred dollars richer with the one shot he allowed himself per kill. He would come back one day and finish the job for the shooting of the survivor. He would have his natural rush for his last hit for at least a couple of weeks.

Ramon was the foreman for Don Luis Montoya's ranch. He had simple values like honor, truthfulness, loyalty, and despising the mean, cruel people who preyed on the weak. The men who hunted good, honest men were the lowest in his book.

He had been collecting information on El Diablo for several years. He probably had more valid information from his friends on El Diablo than any law officer. When he'd heard about Nate being the target for some shooter who never missed, he remembered the great marksman- El Diablo.

My sixth sense had come alive when I'd heard about Nate, and for a few seconds, I'd had a vivid picture of El Diablo. The short, drooped-over figure dressed in black hadn't surprise me. The fact that no one ever remembered him had been a surprise.

Ramon and I had come to the same conclusion at the same time. We would have to take care of El Diablo before he could get a shot at Nate. We had the perfect setup. The Devil was in for a surprise.

El Diablo snapped the case together and started to get up. He looked to his right, and saw Ramon standing there. He glanced to the left and looked me straight in the eye. Ramon took his red handkerchief out of his pocket with his left hand and waved it. A red flag appeared in the doorway of Nate's casa. They were all right there.

I nodded at El Diablo and said, "Not a bad shot if you are shooting at a dummy. I wonder how good you are with someone shooting back at you."

El Diablo was in a daze. He had no idea what was going on. It was the first time things had not gone right for him. He saw that neither of us had a gun in our hands. He might be able to take both of us. As soon as he thought it, he rejected it. It would be a certain death. He had to wait until he had better odds. He was not ready to die. After all, one of the men he had killed for would certainly step forward and help him.

Nate came walking up. "So this is the terrible El Diablo! He looks and smells terrible right now. He's going be the laughingstock of Santa Fe when the hanging judge gets through with him."

All of us were shocked when a tear ran down El Diablo's cheek. His sniper rifle had made him feel special and unbeatable. When they took it out of his hands, he collapsed. It was all that held him up. He was ridiculed during the ride into Santa Fe. The word spread in front of them. "El Diablo arrested." He was only a short man with a short life in front of him. He could not stop crying.

El Diablo stood up in his cell and stretched. It was two weeks later, and he had settled in. It was almost like having friends. Strangely enough, the tears shed by El Diablo made him more likeable.

He climbed up on the front of his bunk to look outside at the sunrise. He rarely missed one, except when they put him in a different cell. The window in front of him was shattered by a bullet that kept on coming until the .50-caliber bullet struck him in the chest. It killed him instantly. A gnarled, old mountain man picked up his buffalo rifle. He rubbed the sight with spit like he always did and put the gun into the rifle boot on his horse. He got up on his horse and rode slowly toward the mountains in front of him. He had avenged his son who had been killed a year before, found with a note in his mouth with the number 280 on it.

The old mountain man thought to himself, *You won that one.* His best guess of his shot was 459 yards. El Diablo was not the best shot in the West. But then the old mountain man and his friends already knew that.

Nate was given the sniper rifle and became good with it.

CHAPTER 9

Johnny Hawk Comanche

He started school in the fourth grade, rapidly caught up, and started working with us as a teacher of the Indians until he went off to an Indian school. He graduated from the special school and then went on to Carlisle University for his master's degree.

He got into politics. He had been lucky. The government had begun a special school for Indians and he excelled in his studies. He saw what the White Apache had meant. Later on, he was elected to the New Mexico Senate and fought for and won many battles for Indian rights. It would be the beginning of a new life for the Comanche. By the time they found out he could not be controlled, he had his own power base.

They did try to assassinate him twice. Two high-ranking government employees were sent to jail, and another killer made the mistake of following Johnny Hawk into an alley to assassinate him. The man who tried this did not come out of the alley.

Johnny Hawk Comanche, as he was called, was one of the most protected men in the country. He was treated with respect by everyone. One day, they would make a movie about him.

CHAPTER 10

Return to Reservation life

Two winters after the sniper's bullet had ended the life of El Diablo, about half of the Comanche stayed out for two weeks in the cold, cold weather while the others stayed out only a few days, lingering as long as possible before seeking warm shelter.

The leaders, four of them, came back knowing they were going to be hung. And they would have been if I had not stopped it.

One of them to be hung was Grizzly Killer. He was now the Comanche chief since Sauktauk had been assassinated. I stopped all the hangings. Ten of the older warriors were sent to Florida. The ones who had been killed in the fight with Rooster, Jodie, and Caleb were identified. The Comanche went back to their reservation. So did Johnny Hawk. I asked him to keep his eyes open while at the reservation. Someone was stirring up every tribe in this area. I was sure it had to do with the company that was given the contract providing food to the reservations. It probably led back to Washington DC. I wanted to find out who it was and why. I wanted to be sure of my facts. It had to be someone high up in the government. I knew someone who would know something about what was going on in this area. Nana was the only surviving Apache chief of Victorio's tribe. He would know, or he would find out and tell me. I would find Nana soon or, more likely, he would find me. It might take another day for me to make a side trip to see Nana, but it would be beneficial to everyone. Don Luis Montoya would know the name people involved in it. Nana would know the local people involved.

None of us knew it right then, but bad trouble was on our way. I reached my father's ranch that evening. He had already heard about the Comanche from Palma, one of Nana's warriors. It was funny how relationships could change. Nana was a bitter enemy of the White Eyes, yet he looked after my family. He would come back by in a couple of hours. He knew I wanted to see him. He was the only Apache chief who was still free. Geronimo had been sent to Florida for three years. He would come back and be a judge on the Apache reservation. A couple of years later, Nana would also be a judge. They wouldn't need to be attorneys; they used the Apache law of right and wrong. It seemed to work better than the settlers' laws. When Geronimo returned, he would join up with Buffalo Bill Cody and Chief Sitting Bull of the Lakota Sioux in a Wild West show. Chief Sitting Bull laughed every time they put on a show. It was not very realistic. He would have killed every one of the whites if they had been really fighting. It made Chief Sitting Bull wonder how they had ever gotten beat by the settlers.

CHAPTER 11

Rooster and Jodie

I got back to Santa Fe late that night and found that two ignorant cowboys had messed their lives up for nothing.

Two ex-cons had gotten them in the position they were in.

It was funny how something trivial could happen in your life that seemed to be of no consequence until it led to a terrible conclusion. It started snowballing and got faster and faster until it got bigger than we were. A few free beers had started Jodie and Rooster on their way to their destruction. Maybe it had even started earlier than that. They had been working for Cowboy several months ago when Rooster decided to go into town. He didn't bother telling Cowboy or anyone else. Rooster was supposed to go out to a line shack and check on any new calves and to check the new barbed-wire fence. He was supposed to relieve Buck Chestnut. He started thinking about a beer, and he stopped by the Round Up Saloon. It was only ten miles out of his way to the line shack. He was there only ten minutes before he got into trouble. It seemed to be his trademark to get into trouble in saloons. Larry Stephens, a four flusher, had had too much to drink. It gave him false courage. Rooster felt kind of mean that morning. Larry Stevens laughed at Rooster when Rooster had to search through all his pockets to find a dime to finish paying for his beer. It was all he had. Rooster called him out. Larry went for his gun, and Rooster beat him by a mile. Being the owner of a big ranch didn't help Larry. Neither did anyone else in the saloon. Rooster was kind to him. He just shot the lobe of his ear off. He could have killed Larry. Instead, he laughed at him.

Jodie was hazing a few steers out of a small draw when Lucky Williams rode up and told him that Rooster had shot part of Larry Steven's left ear off in a fight. Rooster later said he was aiming for Larry's right ear. Peter put Rooster in jail. Larry and his two buddies were inside the Perfect Hand Saloon waiting for Rooster to be released from jail so they could kill him. Larry had a man watching the jail so Rooster could not slip out.

Jodie jerked his horse around and struck out for town and the jailhouse.

Lucky tried to stop him by saying, "Don't you think you better tell Mr. Cowboy about this?" Maybe Jodie heard Lucky and it didn't register, or maybe he was so worried about Rooster he didn't care. At any rate, Jodie spurred his horse and took off for town. Cowboy's ranch was only fifteen miles from Santa Fe.

He rode up to the jailhouse and ran into it. Peter almost shot him. He didn't shoot him because he was expecting Jodie. Rooster, the cause of all this excitement, was lying on the bottom bunk, sound asleep. Rooster could sleep anytime, anyplace.

Jodie almost had a stroke he was so mad at Rooster. Peter had put Rooster in jail for his protection.

He was not under arrest. Rooster woke up and smiled at Jodie. It made Jodie madder. Peter opened the drawer to his desk and handed Rooster his gun belt.

When the man watching the jail saw Jodie ride in, he went and told Larry Stevens since they now had to face Jodie and Rooster. Larry figured he needed one more man. Robert Olson agreed to help for twenty dollars, paid in advance. He had a grudge against Jodie anyway. Jodie had stolen his girl at one of the few dances held on the nearby ranches.

The four men walked over to the street facing the jail. They fanned out. Jodie and Rooster came out the door and onto the wooden sidewalk before they saw Larry and his men. Rooster slid sideways a few steps. Jodie moved a few steps the other way. They were about to start the fracas when they heard the sound of horses approaching. It was Cowboy and two of his men.

Cowboy had become well known for his toughness and his honesty. He told Larry, "If you want to fight Rooster right now by yourself, you can do so." Larry blanched. He had lost the argument yesterday when he'd laughed at Rooster because he couldn't afford a beer. It had gotten him a clipped ear. He knew Rooster was faster with a gun than he was. Larry might have been a coward, but he was no dummy. He decided a notched ear was not so bad after all. He and his men left. Cowboy gave Rooster and Jodie ten dollars each, saying, "It is more than you deserve or have earned."

He told the two cowboys, "You are fired. One reason is for leaving the herd with only one rider, and two is for not telling me you had a problem. Three is because you are both too dumb and lazy to be trusted." As he finished saying this, he remembered his year down in Mexico. He hadn't been a lot different from them back then.

Larry quickly pulled out with his men. He asked Robert for the money he had paid him. Robert refused. He had done what he was told to do. Larry couldn't beat Robert's draw either, so he rode out of town without looking at anyone. The word passed fast enough. He was not looked up to anymore. No one would ride for a man into danger if he was a coward.

Jodie and Rooster lost their jobs at two more ranches, and they were down to their last dollar between them. Worse than that, they had no place to stay for the winter that was almost here. Cowboys earned a place to stay in a bunkhouse with two hot meals a day by working hard during the summer. The two of them could stop at the ranches a few times to eat if they were passing through. They would be cut off after a few feedings. Ranch owners did not run charities for bums. They also didn't want lazy cowboys to think they could get fed even if they didn't work. It was called riding the chow line.

It was their misfortune that Blaze and Lance rode into town the day before Jodie and Rooster did.

Both of them knew the mean-looking cowboys were trouble. Fate now stepped in. They were hooked. They sold their souls for a few bottles of beer. However, in all truthfulness, they would have been willing to help them for even fewer bottles of beer.

The two mean-looking cowboys sat down with Rooster and Jodie. They offered to buy them a beer and continued to buy beer for them. After five or six beers, Rooster and Jodie felt no pain. They had missed their beer, and no one bought any for them anymore since they would never be able to return the favor. This was like money from heaven. Sometimes you got what you deserved, and other times, you just had bad luck. Rooster and Jodie had earned their bad luck by not trying to get jobs. It happened to them all the time.

After a couple of hours, the two mean-looking cowboys told them, "We are planning on robbing McGregor's store tomorrow morning. We want you to hold our horses while we are in the store. No one will be suspicious of you."

Jodie thought about their share of the money. It would get them through the winter. The pending robbery of McGregor's store made Jodie a nervous wreck. This morning seemed to come early to Jodie. He hadn't slept at all. The ex-cons had promised not to hurt anyone. Both Mr. McGregor and the marshal were out of town. Jodie was lazy, but he knew this might get him killed. He had never done anything like this before. He thought to himself, *How come I always seem to wind up in a mess like this? Rooster and me are not bad or mean.*

Then he made a mental confession that startled him: *I guess it's because we're just like Mr. Cowboy said.*

When Rooster Mitchell and he had had a few drinks with the mean-looking cowboys in the Palace Saloon last night, they'd known the two men were trouble. After two or three drinks, they hadn't cared. They would have gone along with anything and anybody. They had been broke for a long time. The beer tasted better than it had ever tasted before. It had been two weeks since they'd had a drink. The dollar between them had bought four beers.

The two lanky cowboys would not look suspicious standing there holding the reins to the horses.

Lance told Blaze, "We will shoot them as we ride away." The two had been out of Yuma Prison for two weeks and had a lot of money to spend. They told Jodie and Rooster how they had robbed a small rancher who had fed them. They had burned the rancher's house down, and they had left the rancher, his wife, and the two children with a barn and two weeks' supply of food. The man at the ranch had worked six years to get his ranch. Sometimes he had to take his family back to Santa Fe if it looked like trouble was coming. It looked like it was starting all over again. With the Comanche out, it might be best to take them in anyway.

Lance had wanted to kill them, but Blaze had talked him out of it. He was pleased with the thirty-eight dollars they got from them. It was the life savings of the rancher.

The rancher would build back. He would never allow any drifters in his house ever again.

They told Jodie and Rooster how they'd had to fight every day in Yuma until they had hurt a lot of cons. Lance had over fifty stitches on his body. Blaze had more. They had lived on the edge and survived.

Over twenty gangs were in the prison. The prisoners joined the various gangs to have protection. Some were worse off in a gang. One member of one of the gangs had crossed over from his gang the Brotherhood to the gang the Family. A guard had found him in a trash can after he had missed his cell check. He had not been killed. They had just wanted to warn him. Blaze was so mean and tough that they had left him alone. Lance had not been that fortunate. They had beaten him up a couple of times. He would never give in. They would have killed him the day Blaze had walked into the latrine.

Four guys had Lance surrounded. Two of them had homemade shanks (knives). Blaze, who had a quick temper, didn't like any of them. Without thinking about it, he smashed one of them in the face with his elbow. He kicked another one between his legs. Lance smashed the one who had turned his head to see what was going on. The fourth guy turned and ran. Blaze and Lance proceeded to break a leg of each of the three men on the floor. Blaze sent out word that if they were attacked in the future, they would start at the top of the gang when they retaliated.

The largest gang by far called themselves "the Devil's Angels." Henry Burton was the gang leader. He sent word back to Lance and Blaze, saying, "You are as good as dead." Henry was six foot four and weighed 294 pounds. He was as mean as you could get. The warden did not like Henry Burton. He still had to work with him until a stronger man came along. Henry had a life sentence. He knew he would never get out. He didn't want to. In Yuma, he was the man, and he loved it. He loved to hear men scream and plead for their lives. He was his own enforcer. Today he was going to make an example of Leon Rathers and maybe Lance and Blaze. Leon had borrowed two dollars from Henry a week ago. He'd lost it in a poker game. He now owed twelve dollars interest, and that didn't included the two dollars that he still couldn't pay. Henry put on the weighted gloves that would split a man's face wide open. He and ten of his bodyguards came down the center aisle in the cellblock. The cons moved away from him and opened up a passage to Leon's cell. He walked very softly for such a big man. He wore a big grin when he saw Leon in his cell. He was going to enjoy this. He approached Leon. Henry waved the bodyguards back. He didn't need any help on this.

Leon was standing, facing the wall. Henry grinned. He was going to enjoy this. He reached out and turned Leon around so he could get a clear shot at his face. He had decided not to kill him. He would mess up his face so badly no one would recognize him. Henry had a split second before he realized that it wasn't Leon standing there. It was Blaze, who said to him, "So long, sucker." He swung the iron pipe smuggled in to him as hard as he could. The iron pipe hit Henry across his nose and face. A second blow settled it. Henry wouldn't die. He would just be a vegetable. His bodyguards were surrounded by fifty cons who jumped on them. Blaze stopped them and settled the inmates down before the guards called it a prison riot. There was a new king in Yuma.

The warden had laughed when he'd heard the story and seen Henry. Since the warden had known it was the gang leaders who really ran the prison, he'd sent word out that he was backing Blaze and Lance. They'd become the real rulers of the prison. They had served their five years in style. They had run the prison better than the warden could. After that, Lance would have jumped off a cliff if Blaze had asked him to do it.

Jodie and Rooster were offered a drink. The next thing they knew, Jodie and Rooster had agreed to help rob McGregor's Mercantile Store.

CHAPTER 12

Mrs. McGregor

Jodie didn't know which one frightened him the most, the ex-cons or the robbery. The two ex-cons had the meanest-looking eyes Jodie had ever seen. They looked right through you, just like a rattlesnake.

Since I was out of town, the robbery seemed like a good idea, at first, to them. The more beer they drank, the better it got. The next morning, as they stood in front of the store, they didn't think it was such a good idea after all. Jodie got sicker by the minute.

About that time, Blaze and Lance rode up to the store. Lance glanced over at Jodie and grinned. Blaze winked at Rooster. Jodie watched them dismount. He was really having a hard time breathing now. He thought he might pass out. He was going to call it off right now. He was too late. Lance and Blaze had already entered the store.

When one of the men came into the store and the other one stayed at the door, Margaret L. McGregor knew the men were up to no good.

She tapped on the counter with a pencil to let Sue, her sister, know they were going to have trouble and to get ready.

She reached under the counter and turned the loaded shotgun she kept there to cover Blaze, who was standing in the door. Sue turned her shotgun toward Lance. Lance was debating whether to kill Sue and Mrs. McGregor. Killing a woman did not bother Blaze or Lance. Lance turned toward Sue. He decided to kill both of them!

Lance waited for Blaze to make his move

Blaze told Mrs. McGregor, "Give me all the money you have." Blaze watched her reach under the counter. He glanced out of the door just as she pulled the trigger on the shotgun under the counter. The first shot tore half the counter off and straightened Blaze up. The second shot blew him out the door right by Jodie. He landed face down in the middle of the street.

The sound of the second shotgun going off filled the store. Lance had reacted to the first shot by Mrs. McGregor. He was not quite quick enough. He and Sue fired at about the same time. Sue shot both barrels of her shotgun at the same time. It knocked her backward against the wall. Lance got off one shot with his pistol. Sue was hard hit as she fell backward. It might have saved her life. Lance flew through the air, hitting the shelves of canned goods behind him. His right side was almost blown away. Canned goods fell off the shelves, almost covering him up

Jodie opened the door just as Mrs. McGregor shot Blaze the second time.

When Lance bounced off the shelves and fell at Jodie's feet, he was a bloody mess.

Jodie had missed the only chance he and Rooster had to call it off. By the time they decided they were not going to help in the robbery, Lance and Blaze were dead. It looked like Sue might be dead also. Jodie was in shock.

Blaze was a crumpled mess in front of the store with part of his side missing. Jodie really was scared now. The one thing you couldn't do in the West was harm a good woman. That made sure you would meet the hanging judge right away if they didn't go on and hang you first. It was for sure they were dead, and he and Rooster would be held responsible for Sue being shot.

Lance's draw and shooting of Sue had been pure reflex. Lance was dead before he realized what a mistake they had made ignoring Sue. When Sue had pulled the trigger of the shotgun, it had been the first time she had ever shot a gun.

Mrs. McGregor had reloaded her shotgun only a few seconds later. In less than five seconds, both ex-cons were dead. Two nice, middle-aged, genteel ladies had killed two of the meanest ex-cons that ever lived.

Jodie, who had entered the store just after Lance was shot, saw Mrs. McGregor calmly standing there with her loaded shotgun. He ran out of the store, yelling, "Let's go. Lance and Blaze are dead, and so is Mrs. McGregor's sister." They galloped out of town, riding full out until their horses began to falter. They rested their horses and then moved along in a fast trot. Ten miles out of town, they joined a trail where the hoof prints of unshod horses were numerous. Neither of them paid any attention to the fact that the tracks were fresh and going the same direction they were going.

I got back to Santa Fe late the next day and was told about the attempted robbery. I'm sure Jodie and Rooster thought they were safe since I hadn't caught them already. I knew neither of them were bad men. They were easily led into trouble. They had worked on several ranches and had been fired because they were lazy. Wintertime was here, and they needed a bunkhouse to spend the winter. Two meals a day was a bonus.

I had just returned from visiting my dad, mom, and Beth. I had stopped by Nate's ranch to spend a couple of hours with him and his wife. Nate had his own ranch now. He'd married Donna, the daughter of Ricardo Perez, one of the vaqueros who work for Don Luis Montoya. Donna was olive skinned and stunningly beautiful. Don Luis had given Nate ten thousand acres. Don

Louis had his vaqueros helping Nate build the second part of his casa. They were living in one room. It was the kitchen and the bedroom combined until they finished the second part. I enjoyed the time I spent with him and his wife. I also saw Cowboy at the ranch we owned together. Cowboy was ready to settle down. So was Beth.

Then the trouble erupted. The Comanche were raiding all over the country. Nate was still working hard to build up their ranch. Donna was staying with her family until the Comanche went back to their reservation. Don Luis would help protect Nate and his wife, who was protected. Soon the ranch would be worth all the time he had spent working on it. He had to be careful. Outlaws, Indians, and perils from nature could show up any day.

I'd give Cowboy my part of the ranch when he and Beth married.

The fifty warriors had stood all they could on the reservation, and they had left it. Nate sent a vaquero to ride out and tell Don Luis Montoya who would then warn all the other families and ask them to warn any other ranches. Everyone would be notified that the Comanche were on the warpath. This was their last hurrah. The Comanche warriors who survived this breakout would be sent to Florida. The people living within an area of two hundred miles of the reservation should get ready for the Comanche who might come their way. Cowboy rode over to stay with my family until the danger was over with. He scattered the herd so the Comanche couldn't find or kill all of them. He could hardly wait. He was going to marry Beth in the spring. Cowboy was scared to death I was going to tell Beth about Rosita. I had some fun with that. I got back to Santa Fe late in the evening. It was already dark.

I spent the night in the hotel we'd bought for Susan. She had hired Madison and Jane Ann Jones to help her run it. They were very good help for her and great company, too. Their father was an attorney who moonlighted as the train station manager. His practice was limited and sluggish since most of the people made their own laws. Their mother worked part-time in the dress shop and taught a special class for the Indians. She was good at both of these.

CHAPTER 13

The Chase

Early the next morning, I started after the two men. I was twenty-three years old, and I was getting a little tired of being the marshal of Santa Fe. In fact, I was just plain tired of the constant problems. I didn't feel good having to put drunken cowboys in jail. Occasionally I had to bash some of them in the head. The two days I was behind Jodie and Rooster made them think they had gotten away. It made them even more careless. I thought they would go north to Taos and then circle back toward Albuquerque, skipping Santa Fe. They didn't head for Taos. They just kept riding toward the land occupied by the fleeing Comanche. They had no idea where they were going.

I had good and bad news for them. I was going to tell them that Mrs. McGregor's sister who had been shot was not going to die. They were not going to hang. The bad news was the Comanche, maybe up to fifty of them, had jumped the reservation. No one knew exactly where they were, but the tracks of the unshod horses in front of us would indicate it might be them. The two cowboys were running to avoid being hung. If the Comanche took them alive, hanging would look good to them. They were going to have to face the hanging judge anyway, but the worst they would get would be a year in Yuma Prison. Yuma never cured any bad men. It just made the bad ones worse. Blaze and Lance were two good examples.

The air was crisp, and I could smell the soft odor of a coming snowstorm. The smell of sage got stronger as it got colder. A lot of folks didn't believe the Apaches could smell a storm coming. I knew they could since I could smell them coming myself. I had found Jodie's and Rooster's tracks about a mile out of town. They had made no effort to hide them. For the last two nights, they had built campfires that would let their smoke and fire be seen. So far, they had been dumb and lucky. It wouldn't last. I would really be surprised if the Indians hadn't gotten to them yet. I was riding my unshod horse (Sugar Foot) so the Comanche wouldn't know I was a White Eye.

About six months ago, I'd seen a drunken cowboy hitting Sugar Foot on his nose with a coiled rope. He had been doing it because he couldn't get up in the saddle. The cowboy had been drunk and cussing a blue streak. I'd finally had to slap him on the side of his head with my gun barrel and arrest him and his two buddies. They'd gotten mad at me for stopping their friend from whipping the horse. The fine for the three men to get out of jail had been fifty dollars. None of them had had any money, so the cowboy had sold me Sugar Foot for fifty dollars. After he had paid his fine, I had the fifty dollars and Sugar Foot. The cowboy had learned a lesson. He had spent a night in jail and had lost his horse too. It hadn't been a good day for him. He'd then had to face his boss. Carlton Murtray owned Evergreen, the spread the three men rode for. He had been ranching about forty years and had earned the right to keep the one hundred thousand acres he had fought for. He was a fair man and a tough one. Later on, I had ridden out to his ranch and talked to him about his cowboys. He'd had a few choice words to say to his men.

I had my moccasins on along with my deerskin coat. They were warm at night and waterproof.

My buffalo waterproof coat kept my bedroll dry. The buffalo hide could be soaking wet outside and dry inside. The outside of the coat shed water so well that it would dry out ten minutes after being soaking wet.

It felt good to have it to sleep under. The glow of the stars sparkled off and on again, even on this cold, wet night. I was Lone Eagle, the White Apache again. I liked it! My senses were sharper. I felt more alive now.

I thought about the two ladies who ran McGregor's. Both of them were typical frontier women, just like hundreds of others living in Santa Fe. They could be a trifle slow sometimes because they enjoyed talking to the customers who liked to talk also. Mrs. McGregor had once made a young man decide not to rob her. On any given day, she would have shot him; however, in this case, just pointing her shotgun at him stopped him from creating a lifetime of trouble for himself and others. Calm under pressure, she had talked him into walking away, promising not to do anything like that again. She had sent him out to Bill Talbot's ranch, and Bill had hired him. He had made Bill a top hand immediately. The young man felt he had been lucky for it to be her he'd approached instead of her husband. He was probably right. Everyone liked Mrs. McGregor and Sue.

A lynch mob had wanted to go with me, but I'd turned them down. The odds were both Jodie and Rooster were dead, killed by the Comanche. There was no sense in letting some of the others get killed, and they would have if I had let them go with me.

Sugar Foot was perfect for this trip. An unshod pony wouldn't create as much attention. A shod pony would get me killed. The unshod horses ridden by Indians lasted long enough except on rough ground, and if they came up lame, the Indians ate them.

They made up for it by having a lot of speed over a short-distance run.

After three days chasing them, I figured Jodie and Rooster were only about an hour in front of me. If they had gone a different route, they might have gotten away. They had to be the luckiest men in the world not to have been killed by the Comanche.

CHAPTER 14

The Fight

The sound of gunshots broke out about a mile in front of me. I got off my horse about a quarter of a mile from where the shots were coming from. It had to be Rooster and Jodie. I slipped up to where they were.

It was the two cowboys. I looked over the small ridge. I could just see what was happening in the narrow canyon below me. I made sure the Comanche did not see me or have a clean shot at me if they did. I made sure I was behind some boulders with small piñon pines in front of them. The trees were stunted being just below the tree line of seven thousand feet where only the hardiest trees could live. The nuts from a piñon pine tree were good to eat.

A small Conestoga (wagon) blocked most of the entry to the small canyon below me. I could see a young boy in the Conestoga. He was ready to fight. I counted fourteen Comanche coming up to the canyon to get into position to attack the ones in the canyon.

It was easy to see their strategy. Some were almost already into position. Five Comanche would go down each side of the canyon. One young Comanche stayed with the horses. Three Comanche were going to climb the bank where I was sitting and get above the trapped men. Two out of the five warriors on the other side would try to find a place on the other side to get a similar shot at the trapped men be low them. If I had not come right then, it would have been a slaughter. Jodie was a little higher than Rooster was. It exposed him more.

The Comanche felt like they had nothing to lose. It was a living death on the reservation, and at least in this battle, they would die an honorable death if they were killed.

I recognized Guitano, one of the best fighters I'd ever met. I'd met him while visiting Sautauk, the Comanche chief. Guitano had Jodie in his sights. Jodie shifted a little and slid behind a boulder. Guitano shot his arrow into the shadow behind the boulder Jodie was behind. Jodie jumped as the arrow tip created a geyser of sparks that flew from where Guitano's arrow hit. I shot Guitano's shoulder just as he saw me. It was not intended as a killing shot, only one to put him out of action. I let him crawl away. Jodie did a quick roll down into the bottom of the canyon. They couldn't see him. I could see everyone. I could see Rooster move over to the right side of the rock he was behind. He was giving Jodie some covering fire.

Rooster's foot was bent at an unusual angle. Rooster and Jodie had shot their horses. The young boy had not shot his horse yet. They knew they could not get away, so they had shot their horses to give them something more to hide behind. They knew they were not going to leave this canyon alive.

I was slightly above them, and I could see the entire scene develop below me.

I hollered to the Comanche below me, saying, "This is Lone Eagle. Come on back to the reservation, and I will make sure you get a fair trial." They knew they would not receive the same justice the settlers did and, in all probability, face much worse. I saw that Grizzly Killer was one of the Comanche. He was wearing chief's clothing. He had replaced Sauktauk. I knew him well. He might consider coming in.

Bullets peppered the rocks around me. I shot twice at the Comanche below me even as they tried to retreat from their position. One Comanche jumped, even though the ledge he was on was fifteen feet off the ground. Shots from Rooster's position got one of the last two coming down from my position. Two Comanche lay in the bottom of the canyon, shot by the three men in their trap. When my shouts alerted them to the Comanche coming down the other side, it gave them a chance. However, some of them had good shots at Rooster, and I could hear the bullets striking him. He was killed instantly. Jodie was caught in a cross fire and was struck by several bullets. He wounded one more Comanche. Jodie, knowing it was me above him, crawled over toward Rooster to try to save him.

The young man in the Conestoga had waited for a good shot. He got it, and Grizzly Killer, who had survived a charge by a mean mother grizzly bear, was wounded by a twelve-year-old boy. I would hate to see my friend Grizzly Killer killed, but no one had any choice in this. I had a good shot at Latanza and took it; seconds later, Latanza grabs his chest and falls in a heap. Jodie rolled over, trying to get one more shot at the last Comanche still fighting. The Comanche shot him in his side with his arrow. Jodie died with one thought. He wished he had been strong enough to call off the robbery of McGregor's store and that the lady who had been shot had not died. The death gurgle started in his throat, and by the time it ceased, Jodie was dead. One dead Comanche had two rifles with him, but he had no bullets that fit his guns. The firing ceased. He didn't need the .44 caliber anymore. My last shot caught him in the throat. The Comanche pulled out. This included Grizzly Killer. They knew Ussen was not on their side this day. They would not die just to prove their bravery. They wanted to live to fight another day.

I moved on down to the canyon floor. It was time for us to move on. They would be back. As I climbed down from the top of the canyon, I saw the remaining four Comanche jump on their horses and ride away. I could have shot two of them, but we had already killed or wounded ten or twelve of them. When I got to Jodie and Rooster, they were dead. We had killed four and wounded six more of them. The young Comanche looking after the horses also escaped. I could have killed him but chose not to. Caleb had handled himself really well. He might have been the difference!

One of the wounded that rode away was Grizzly Killer, my old Comanche friend who had earned his name by fighting a mother grizzly bear with only his knife and lived to tell about it

This was his story too.

CHAPTER 15

Grizzly Killer

I thought back to my years with the Apaches. They were good years for me. I had been given the name "Little Warrior" first because I'd showed no fear when captured. I'd been nine years old. I'd become a warrior with honor. I'd received my Apache name, Lone Eagle, from Ussen while I had been high on a Sandia Mountain peak with bolts of lightning striking all around me. I had been fifteen when I'd become a warrior. Apache warriors didn't pick their names. Ussen (God) did it for them. If you did something special, you changed your name. Apache warriors might get four or five names changes as they got older. The name told you something about the warrior.

A good example of winning a name was the story of how the name "Grizzly Killer" had been given to One Who Talks Too Much. He was a Comanche warrior in Sautauk's tribe. He'd become a shaman (medicine man) and chief when Sauktauk had been killed. He had a small wound where Caleb had shot him in the arm. He'd gotten back to the Comanche reservation soon after I'd pardoned the ones who had left the reservation. He believed like I did that the reservations could govern themselves. I had appointed him as one of the reservation judges. He was a good Comanche warrior, and he became a legend in his own time. He was still my friend. The reason for him having the name "One Who Talks Too Much" was obvious. Life was good to him. He was able to provide food for his family, and he had just returned from a successful raid stealing horses from the Navajo. He had been hunting about an hour. He always looked forward to a day of hunting. He had not seen any game yet, but it didn't matter. He was happy just being out hunting. He heard a noise in the brush in front of him. It wasn't much of a noise, so he figured it must be rabbits or some other small animals feeding on something they had found. He tiptoed up to the place the noise was coming from. He parted the bushes. Two young grizzly cubs were on the other side of the bushes play fighting. They had dug up a hill of black ants and had finished eating them. They had dirt all over them. When he parted the bushes, the two cubs looked up and saw him. They had never seen a human before. As taught by their mother, they squealed and took off toward the bushes. He scared them so badly, they continued squealing as they ran in the general direction of their mother. The mother grizzly bear was the fiercest defender of her young in the animal kingdom. The female grizzly was approximately two-thirds the size and weight of a male grizzly who had been known to kill and eat bear cubs. Most of the time, the female grizzly would attack the male so fiercely that the male would turn and run from her and find something else to eat. In some cases, the male would win the fight, but he would have to kill the female to get to her cubs. She was feeding on wild berries in the bushes about twenty yards from him when she heard her cubs squealing.

She never hesitated. She charged him, coming out of the berry bushes as fast as she could run. The claws in her paws, which were normally retracted, opened up on her first step toward him. One Who Talks Too Much saw the mother grizzly bear bearing down on him. He only had enough time to shoot two of his arrows into the bear. It didn't even slow her down. He didn't hit any place that would kill her. The grizzly was as fast as lightning, and she was on him before he could turn to run. All his arrows had done was make the grizzly mad. He dropped his bow and arrows and drew his knife. The grizzly bear hit him with her paw. It ripped half of his coat off and gave him some deep cuts on his arm. It knocked him ten feet away from her. It saved his life. He didn't have much of a chance, but he got his knife out and held it, pointing straight up as the grizzly pounced on him. She landed on One Who Talks Too Much chest so she could gut him with her massive claws. The knife wound made her let him go for a few seconds. The bear's claws cut him on his arm and shoulder instead of his stomach as she rolled off of him. The bear's weight had forced the knife deep into her heart. She knew she was mortally wounded. The fight was still not over. The warrior managed to get up on his feet. The bear was so mad that she swatted at him again and missed. Grizzly Killer had no way to escape her. He stepped inside her long arms feeling a burning fire on his back where the grizzly got him again. He got his knife in a position he could stab her. He stabbed the grizzly in her neck, severing the aorta.

He pulled his knife free again. The handle was so slippery with blood that he dropped it. Blood squirted all over him and the bear. The cubs shrieked and cried out. The grizzly turned and walked away from One Who Talks Too Much to check on her cubs. She was dying, but she still wanted to get the man who threatened her cubs.

She turned back to Grizzly Killer. One step away from him, she collapsed. So did Grizzly Killer, as he would be called from then on. The grizzly's claws would have ripped him to pieces, and the great jaws on the grizzly would have crushed his head if the cubs had not squealed out. They would be eating him. As bad as he was hurt, Grizzly Killer pried the massive jaws apart and cut out as many teeth as he could. Then he removed the claws so he could make a necklace out of them later. It would be good medicine for him. He would have the scars on his chest, back, and arms to prove how close he'd come to being a meal for the grizzly bears. He was bleeding profusely. His arm, chest, back, and legs had deep cuts in them. The bear had great courage, and she died still trying to get at One Who talks Too Much. He thought the bracelet would give him the strength and courage of the great bear. Who knew? After that, he was stronger and braver.

He knew he had to get help soon or he would die. He was surprised that the cubs did not run away. They came over to him and rubbed against him. They were young, and since they had never seen a human before, they were no longer afraid of him. They squealed and adopted him right away. They started licking the blood coming out of his wounds. One Who Talks Too Much thought that they were going to attack him. He knew he was too weak to defend himself. His knife was laying on the ground somewhere. It became obvious the cubs were no longer afraid of him. One of the strange things about this was the blood they licked off him didn't make them go wild and try to kill him. They did some things that they had never been taught. It was part of their inherited knowledge. Licking a wound cleaned some of the germs also. Grizzly Killer shooed them away from him. They moved over a few feet and sat there, waiting for him to lead them. He cut up his shirt and the rest of his coat to staunch the flow of blood as best as he could. He knew he had to get back to his camp before he bled to death. The cubs had cleaned his wounds a little when they licked them. One Who Talks Too Much started walking back to his village with the cubs following along behind him. Time after time, they almost knocked him down as they tried to get closer to him. He stopped when he saw some moss on the north side of a tree. The moss stopped most of the bleeding.

Kenta was out hunting too. He heard Grizzly Killer coming. He stepped behind a tree and waited. He had his repeating rifle ready. He couldn't believe his eyes. One Who Talks Too Much staggered out of the brush and walked toward him. He was a terrible sight. He had blood all over him. As Kenta stepped out to grab him to keep him from falling, he saw the bear cubs. They hissed at him to tell him to stay away from their newly adopted parent. Kenta pointed his gun into the air and shot three times. It was the signal that one of them needed help. The cubs ran a short distance away from them when he shot his gun. Then they came back to where Grizzly Killer was and brushed against him continually. They got behind him, bawling because they were hungry and scared. It helped them to be with Grizzly Killer, the one who almost had become their meal. In five minutes, seven warriors surrounded them. One look at Grizzly Killer and they grabbed him up and took off for their camp. The warriors were astounded that the cubs wanted to stay close to Grizzly Killer, who told the warriors the cubs were his now that their mother was dead. The two cubs fussed because they were having a hard time keeping up with the ones running with Grizzly Killer

He was hanging between two warriors that switched positions every so often with the other four warriors. One warrior back tracked the bloody warrior back to where Grizzly Killer had his fight with the bear. Blood was everywhere. The bear had dug up the ground with her great paws. She was over eight feet tall and weighed over five hundred pounds. The women came and skinned the bear. They did it much better than the warriors. They skinned the bear and wrapped up the bear meat in the fur. Each of them loaded as much as they could carry. More women would come to get the rest of the meat.

As they entered, the village people came out of their teepees to see what all the clatter was about. They were astounded. The two cubs knocked over food pots, scattered campfires, and charged the dogs to keep them away from Grizzly Killer. The village was amazed the cubs were willing to fight anyone who got close to Grizzly Killer. The women started arriving with their herbs and plants. A couple of warriors wanted to shoot the cubs only to be stopped by Grizzly Killer.

He told them, "The cubs are now part of my family. They saved my life." After saying that, he slid away into darkness. His wife and most of the women spent the night boiling soup, hot water, and the herbal medicine he would take all through the night. They gave him something mixed with aloe to make him sleep while they sewed him up. Early the next morning, he woke up to the worse squalling he had ever heard. The two cubs were tied to a tree next to his teepee. They wanted food and wanted to be untied. It was the only time in years he had slept past the dawn. He got up very slowly and very carefully. He knew the best thing to do for wounds was to get up and walk, but he had to be extra careful. His wife, Bonita (Pretty Woman), always had a pot of soup on. He walked outside over to where the cubs were tied. He picked up two bowls and filled them with the meaty soup. He sat them down in front of the bears and sat between them. Bonita brought him a bowl of soup and got one for her and sat down with them. He told her the story of how the cubs had saved his life. The cubs were very hungry, and between Grizzly Killer, Bonita, and the two cubs, they ate three days' supply of food. All of her stored edible vegetables had been added to the pot with a couple of gallons of water. After the soup was gone, the bear cubs licked and licked the empty bowls where their new supply of food had come from. They didn't understand why the food didn't keep coming to their bowls. As long as Grizzly Killer was with them, they would sit quietly. They adopted Bonita also. At first, they would cry so pitifully they won Bonita over in a short time. He never did convince her that the cubs were taking advantage of her. They were smart critters. Grizzly Killer was not so easy. He had already decided they would have to earn their way. With him, they did as he told them to. As the cubs grew, they learned to kill enough for the two of them, Grizzly

Killer, and Bonita. Another legend was born. Grizzly Killer was thought to be a special shaman. The cubs grew and grew. They obeyed Grizzly Killer just like they would have obeyed their own mother if she were alive. Grizzly Killer taught the cubs not to tear up anything. The cubs liked Bonita, and they would walk down to the stream to get water with her. She would load two water bags on each cub. They would walk back to camp with one of the bears on each side of her. The cubs ran down rabbits, deer, and occasionally a buffalo. They also could outrun Grizzly Killer and all the other warriors. Grizzly Killer always gave them a portion of their kill. He cut off their part of the meat they had killed and put it on the ground as their reward. Sometimes he made them wait to eat together with him and Bonita. It took a while to do this. The older Apaches told Grizzly Killer that one day; they would revert to being grizzly bears and kill or hurt some or all of them.

Grizzly Killer had seen it coming. He knew the bears needed to live their own natural lifestyle. They needed to be far away from people. His reputation grew and grew. The cubs were three or four years old by then.

The cubs' reputation and size grew. They weighed over four hundred pounds and were about eight feet tall. As it was in nature, when the two male grizzly cubs became full grizzly bears, they didn't get along with each other. They had to be separated. They were too big and too dangerous. One of the camp dogs bit one of the bears when the bear ate his food. The bear disemboweled the dog. The smell of blood was too strong. They ate the dog. Grizzly Killer knew the bears could not be trusted anymore, so he thought about taking them north into the land of the boiling springs. He decided he needed to do it quickly. It was a hard decision for Bonita, even though she agreed it was necessary. It was the beginning of fall when they left to go north. Grizzly Killer was worried about meeting a band of Indians on the way up to the springs. His reputation as a bear killer and bear tamer preceded him.

He was always welcome by the Sioux and the other tribes with open arms. The bears were nervous at first, but they learned to like it since they were fed well every time they met some tribe. Grizzly Killer was asked to demonstrate the fight with the female Grizzly and to show his scars. He wore his necklace of teeth and claws proudly. He was treated as a shaman. Everyone sat in silence when he spoke. He was always treated with respect.

He noticed that the cubs imitated him. When he got behind bushes and trees, they did too. When he walked without making any more noise than he could help, they did too. It was funny how two eight-foot bears could hide as well as he could. They dodged a band of Lakota Sioux who were on the warpath. It took over two weeks to get to the Land of Boiling Waters. When they arrived, they marveled at the sight of steam rising from the water. It had already turned cool. He had to try the water out. He tested several small lakes, finding them too hot. He found where the hot water flowed into a small creek. The water was perfect. He had to laugh every time the cubs tested the water as he did. When he sat down in the creek, they watched him a minute or so before they tested it by sitting down next to him. The water was perfect.

He separated them by leaving each one on their side of a lake. He was surprised they did it without any fuss. It was beginning to get colder. Signs of other grizzlies were abundant. They would have to fight their own battles for the right to live in the woods and survive. He knew he could do nothing to help them. They were bigger than almost all the other bears. It helped for them to be as big as they were. Grizzly Killer knew he had to get back to his own village. He left them and rode west a few miles to keep them from following him. He then went back to his village. They might have tried to come back if he had not made his trail a different way to go back home. In a few weeks, it would be the time for them to hibernate. They would need to eat heavily so they could have enough food to hibernate the cold winter. They had done that for winters outside Grizzly Killer's village. One day not too long after Grizzly Killer had left, the bears were hunting, and they met in the woods. One of them brought down a deer. They shared the large deer. It was the last time they shared food. After eating the deer, the brothers split up to go into hibernation. When they woke up, both of them went in different directions. They never saw each other again. Each of them found mates and started their own families. Both of them had several fights with other male grizzlies. They won most of them and moved their territory when they lost one. Yellowstone Park still had the buffalo running free and the boiling waters along with Old Faithful spewing hot water high into the air every few hours. It still took your breath away. Nature taught them how to survive. Grizzly Killer wondered about them many times, and the two bears often stuck their noses up in the air searching for the smell of Grizzly Killer, Bonita, and each other. After a few minutes, they would go back to doing what grizzly bears did. Grizzly Killer knew he was right to take them north, but it still hurt him and his wife. The bears roamed the Land of Boiling Waters, totally happy with themselves. Grizzly Killer was wounded in the battle with two cowboys and a young boy. It was a good fight. He was remembered as a brave warrior for his role in Nana's battle with the Mexicans, but he was better remembered for his fight with the grizzly. His story was told many times at the campfires.

The only other Apache known to have survived a fight with a grizzly with just his knife called himself Bear. A year later, his horse shied at a snake on the trail going up the mountain, and he and Bear went off the side of the pass.

I remembered that after a few years, I had become a true Apache and followed Apache customs. They were good customs. Now it was the Indians who must follow some customs of the settlers.

It was again time to finish with my destiny and Ron Jedrokoski. The Lakota Sioux had to run north into Canada for a while. The large tribes of Crow, Blackfeet and Comanche, Apache, Navajo, and most of the other tribes would never challenge the US government again. Their day in the sun was over.

CHAPTER 16

Comanche Surprise

We thought it was over. We almost made a fatal mistake. We had missed one Comanche. Jodie and Rooster were dead. The Conestoga wagon blocked half of the entrance to the small canyon. The wounded warrior climbed around the wagon, hidden by Caleb's dead horse. The Comanche had been shot earlier and had just come to. He wanted one last shot before he died. He took a step toward the wagon. He wanted to show his courage, and he thought all of them could be dead. Caleb and I both shot him. Either shot would have killed him. The Comanche staggered, put his hand on his chest, and toppled over. I had changed the odds and the results. I got Sugar Foot and rode down the small trail into the canyon. A wagon could not have made it to the top of the canyon from either side. I heard a horse whinny and figured the Comanche had left some horses away from the entrance to the canyon. The three left in the war party would be back. From the looks of it, Jodie and Rooster and the one in the wagon had fought pretty well. They had the best of it. Six dead Comanche were on the ground. Two more had been wounded and soon died. They had expected me to kill them. Four Comanche rode off while two of the wounded crawled away. Caleb and I had killed the last one. Two of the three Comanche who had not been shot were going to go back to the larger war party and get them. Soldado (soldier), one of the three who had been wounded but survived, decided he could ride his horse around the canyon and maybe get one of us with his last arrow. The other two were to ride as fast as they could back to the main camp and bring the warriors after them. One Who Thinks Too Much and his horse had been hit by stray bullets. He continued on his ride back to camp, but his horse didn't make it. Soldado had to pick up the warrior without a horse and was filled with so much hate that he forgot what he was doing. He didn't check on his friend until he fell off the horse. He had bled to death. Soldado got another name—One Who Forgets His Friends in Battle. It took years and his rescue of a young Comanche from the Sioux for him to overcome the name.

I had a vision of the beginning of the battle between Rooster, Caleb, and the Comanche. My sixth sense came back to me with a rush. I turned toward the wagon and hollered out, "Don't shoot. I'm the marshal of Santa Fe." A young boy stood up and walked toward me. He kept his rifle trained on me. He was not afraid of me, but he was careful. I walked on down the canyon and looked at the bodies of Jodie, Rooster, and Charles Rayborn, who was the boy's uncle. The young boy was named Caleb. He had fought well, and the Comanche would probably not have mutilated him. If he had survived, they would have taken him with them.

With my sixth sense, I could see what had happened to Jodie, Rooster, and the young boy. The two cowboys had ridden out of the small canyon and had been about a mile from it. They had been riding slowly when they had seen the boy (his uncle had been in the back of the wagon) coming toward them in an old small Conestoga wagon pulled by the boy's saddle horse. During their journey in a wagon train, the boy had been off hunting. His uncle was down with a fever. He was lying in the bed of the wagon. The two mules that had been pulling the wagon were gone. They had been stolen. They were told they would have to leave the wagon train because everybody in the wagon train figured Charles Brantly had yellow fever. He was about gone. Caleb and Charles were lucky, although they didn't know it. Six hours after they left the wagon train, the Comanche killed almost everybody in it. Jodie and Rooster rode up to him.

A few minutes later, the horse staggered and almost fell as he tried to pull the wagon up the sandy incline. The band of fourteen Comanche came over a rise and saw them. They raced after them. The outlaws jerked their horses around, grabbed the reins of the horse pulling the wagon, and rode as fast as the winded horse pulling the wagon could run. He had pulled hard and didn't have much left in him.

They made it to the entrance of the canyon before the horse collapsed. Rooster was unlucky.

One of the shots fired at him hit his horse. The horse was game and had run the mile back to the canyon before he collapsed. When the horse fell, Rooster jumped off, turning a somersault. The horse didn't fall on him, but he broke his ankle when he slammed into the ground. Jodie immediately turned around and went back for Rooster, who couldn't walk. His ankle was shattered. He had grabbed his rifle as he fell and was slowly trying to pull himself up. The Comanche were right behind them. It was too late to get away. The Comanche had them. Jodie grabbed Rooster and his rifle and threw him behind a boulder. Then he turned and shot as fast as the seventeen-shot Winchester could. Two of the Comanche fell off their horses, and the rest turned to the right side of the canyon. It had some boulders that gave them some cover. The Comanche were not in a hurry now. Jodie and Rooster and the two in the wagon could not escape. The White Eyes knew it. They killed their horses to give them more cover.

No one said it, but all of them knew it was their last stand. Jodie propped Rooster up and found him a position where he could see down the canyon. The Comanche split up and began to move toward the trapped foursome. Jodie changed position and got up on one of the boulders that had a small niche on top of it. He could see out of the side of the boulder without being seen. He waited until they were right below him. His shot surprised the Comanche. Juhari was killed instantly. So was one of Juhari's friends. The Comanche scattered, and now Jodie had a real problem. Several paths led up to his position.

Jodie dropped back down to where Rooster lay. It was as good a place as any to die. Rooster had shot the heel off a Comanche who thought he was hidden. Rooster had been hit in the arm. He put his kerchief around the wound and continued to fire at the Comanche. As their ammunition began to run out, they were more selective with their shots. The two in the wagon were shooting also.

An arrow got Jodie. It went through his chest. He cut the head of the arrow off and got Rooster to pull it out. He plugged the holes by cutting his kerchief in half. Jodie knew he only had a few minutes to live and only a few bullets left. The Comanche shot the wagon to pieces. The young boy had gotten behind some rocks and was safe for the moment. Charles Rayborn, his uncle, who was already sick with fever, stayed in the wagon. He was hit several times and was dead. Jodie called out to the young boy and told him to try to get away. Caleb Webster would not leave his uncle or the two cowboys. The Indians began their crawl forward to better positions. Rooster was hit with a ricochet and died instantly. Jodie threw Caleb Rooster's rifle, got all the ammunition Rooster had, and ran over to where Caleb was.

Kuntas had waited for this one shot, and he hit Jodie and spun him around. Jodie crawled over to Caleb, knowing he was hard hit and only had a few minutes left. He died a couple of minutes later, thinking what a shame it was, that Caleb was too young to be in this mess, and how dumb he and Rooster were. As I lay behind the stand of piñon pines, I knew if I had been a few minutes earlier, I might have been down there with the outlaws. I might have made difference. It had never been a question of if but when the Comanche would see their tracks. It was a dead certainty they would. It had been a small war party that had caught them. The fight had lasted too long for it to be a big one. The larger war party must have been a few miles away. My vision ended. Rooster and Jodie had paid for their carelessness.

Jodie had thought about killing himself, but Caleb had made him change his mind. They were heroes to some degree. Both were dead. Jodie had been hit twice with bullets. The Comanche were game. They had suffered a great loss in this battle, but they still wanted Caleb's scalp. I waited for the Comanche to climb up to where they thought they would get a good shot at Caleb. They were totally unaware I was above them. I got the first two, and the others just disappeared.

CHAPTER 17

Back to Santa Fe

We had to move fast since the Comanche would be back in less than an hour. I heard the horses whinny again. I had only a short distance to go to them. I got two of the horses. I got one for Caleb and one for our supplies. Caleb got his bedroll, his blankets, two rifles, and a pistol from the wagon. He got what the little money they had. I cut thick slices of meat from one of the dead horses. I took some over to Caleb, who refused it. I ate mine. Finally, Caleb took a bite of his, and since he was really hungry, he took another bite and finished most of his. I had eaten raw meat many times while living as an Apache. It was amazing how much raw meat an Indian could eat. I cut me another slice of the meat. I knew we might not have a chance to eat while we were running from the Comanche. I left eight horses in the canyon. That would give them something to think about.

Caleb told me, "My uncle was taking me to California to my grandfather's ranch." Tony Rakestraw was his grandfather. Caleb's uncle had known he was in bad shape. He would have been glad to know I was there with Caleb. Caleb set fire to the wagon after getting what he needed from it. We had a hard time getting all of the stuff on one of the Indian ponies. The pony was not used to the smell of settlers. Caleb looked at his horse that had given his all while pulling the wagon even though he was all used up. Like all Westerners, he loved his horse.

The weather was changing, getting much colder. The sky had turned slate gray, and the wind had picked up. I kept the Comanche horse on a string by tying a rope to the tail of my horse and to the head of the Comanche horse. Caleb had gotten the rope from the wagon. The horses were frisky, but Sugar Foot became their leader and they settled down.

We'd put Charles, Rooster, and Jodie in the wagon. We didn't have time to bury them. In a few minutes, we had a roaring fire. We had a small keg of coal oil that burned fiercely. It was time to move out. Later on, the coyotes would come and clean up the bodies.

Big snowflakes began falling, and in less than an hour, visibility was almost gone. We had to find shelter. I remembered a cave nearby, and although I had never looked inside it, I knew it would be better than nothing. I left the Comanche horses in the canyon. I figured the Comanche would stop chasing us when they saw them. Most Indians didn't care whom they took their revenge on.

Someone in the future would face the wrath of the Comanche. They would get their revenge on the next people in the next battle they fought. We started home in the deep snow. Some of the low places had accumulated up to five or six feet of snow. We took turns breaking the trail. We found the cave about an hour before dark. We almost didn't see it.

We had Sugar Foot, Caleb's horse, and the horse with supplies on it. I put them in the back of the cave. I covered the front entrance with a blanket that I stuck in the cracks at the top of the cave. Someone before us had worked hard chipping out the cracks. Whoever he was he had spent a good bit of time in the cave. A stack of wood was near the back of the cave. Lucky for us, the wind was blowing away from the opening. I got some of the wood and pine needles. Using the flint rock I always carried and my bowie knife, I soon had a good fire going. The pine needles made it easier to start the fire. Caleb collected some more pine needles under the trees close to us. It only took a few minutes since the wood in the cave was perfectly dry. It would burn well in the fire. We would do the same thing before we left. We would leave a large stack of wood in the back of the cave. To start the fire, I put a small stack of dry needles in the shape of a teepee. I hit the edges of the flint rock with the blade of my bowie knife. The sparks flew, and a spark finally caught up in the pine needles. I blew on it until I got a small fire going. The flint rock had saved a lot of people. We added bigger and bigger pieces of wood until we finally had a good fire going. Caleb brought in another armful of wood and a pine limb that had fallen recently. The pine limb would burn hot because of the rosin in it. Caleb cut a lot of the pine needles off the branches and put them in the back of the cave. I piled up some rocks to reflect the heat back into the cave. The wind had died, and the horses were used to winter weather, so I went out and found a big tree that had only a little snow under it. I put them under an overhanging tree that sheltered the horses from the snow. I would check on them again that night. I rigged a picket line to hold the horses, although I knew Sugar Foot would not try to leave. I knew they would like being in the open air instead of the cave. I gave them the rest of the corn I had packed for them. Large pines were fairly common here, so we hacked off some more limbs. We had enough wood to last the night. I told Caleb, "When we leave tomorrow, we will leave wood for the next one who stays in the cave." We drank a couple of cups of coffee apiece. It was made with melted snow. I gave him the last of my pemmican.

Sugar Foot assumed the role of the leader right away. Caleb tried to stay awake, but in just a few minutes, he was sound asleep. The warm cave had helped him cave in. He needed more sleep than I did. Snow had covered the blanket in front of the cave except for the smoke hole. The smoke coming out of the hole would not be noticed unless someone was close by. The temperature inside had hovered around thirty five. The temperature outside was much colder. It finally got too cold even for our horses. I went out, got them, and I put them in the back of the cave. It was probably still close to freezing in the cave, but it sure beat being outside. All in all, we spent the night comfortably warm. I woke up at what should have been sunrise. The falling snow made the sun slow in making its appearance. I fed the fire and put on the pot of water (melted snow) and when it was boiling, I dumped yesterday's coffee grounds in it. The coffee was weak, but it was better than nothing. We stayed a short while after sunrise. I took some ashes from the dying fire and made dark circles under our eyes. I cautioned Caleb not to look directly at the sun or the white snow long without looking away or he could be snow blind. We were about ready to leave. I made a torch and walked to the back of the cave to make sure we had left enough wood for the next one to use the cave. I saw something written on the back wall of the cave. A few minutes more, and the fire would have gone out and we would have missed it. The name Kit Carson and the number of the year, 1779, carved on the back wall. I had heard of him. Everybody had heard of him I guess. We also saw a picture of a great bear as tall as two men carved into the wall. He was fighting twelve men who surrounded him. He was bloody all over where they had used their spears on him. Three men were lying on the ground, looking all broken up. There was no doubt that it was a grizzly bear. Another drawing showed a medicine man helping two warriors get well. One drawing had men wearing armor and fighting the Indians. Seeing the wall was like reading a book. It was a true depiction of the past. I hoped no one ever destroyed the drawings. The drawings were reminders that this land had been inhabited by many different kinds of people over the past two hundred years. The wall was a good lesson in history. It showed a good part of the Indian way of life. Only the settlers destroyed everything they touched. This had been a holy cave used by the shamans. They had used it to treat the wounded and sick. The drawings of shamans lined the wall showing how far back the cave had been used. Using one shaman per thirty years, it would go back to the early 1600s.

It had quit snowing, and it was time to go home. It was going to snow a lot more in a few hours, so again we took turns breaking the trail. The further down we got, the easier it was to break the snow. Caleb never complained, and he kept up with me. We pushed it and got back to Santa Fe late that night.

CHAPTER 18

Caleb Meets Susan

We were hungry, dirty, and cold when we got to the hotel.

I had been thinking of something all the way back. I wanted Susan to meet Caleb.

Caleb kind of hung back until he saw Susan. She had that effect on all the males she came in contact with. She took charge of Caleb. She gave him a room and fixed him a tub full of hot water that felt great to him. She gave him clean clothes that someone had left at the hotel. They were a little big on Caleb, but he liked them anyway. After he bathed himself and put on the new clothes, he came down the stairs. Susan fed us leftovers. Mealtime had passed.

We had roast beef, potatoes, biscuits, and apple pie. Caleb couldn't believe we ate this good all the time. That was why our hotel stayed full most of the time.

I had been thinking of Caleb, so I made Susan sit down with us while we talked. Susan had some help. Madison and Janie Ann Jones lived in the hotel with their parents. Their mother, Amy, had run a dress shop across from the hotel until the new school had opened in late May. Amy really liked to teach. Mike, their father, worked as an attorney. We were almost civilized enough to settle some problems without the use of guns. Mike had one motto: do what is right! They stayed at the hotel at a much cheaper rate. They were the kind of people Santa Fe needed. Susan loved having females she could talk to.

Maddie and Janie helped in the hotel. I told Susan that I had been thinking of Caleb, and I would like for him to stay with us or he could stay with the Bakers. It was his choice. It only took a couple of seconds for Caleb to choose us. He had a smile from ear to ear. Until we found his parents or he found someone else, he could stay with us. He relaxed. He and Susan became friends that minute.

The coolness on the back of my neck was still there. I walked over to the jail to see if Bill had had any trouble while I'd been gone. Everybody knew what had happened to Rooster and Jodie. They were now heroes and got more respect dead than they had alive. A lot of people thought Rooster and Jodie had saved Mrs. McGregor's and Sue's lives.

I woke up the regular time, about six. As I walked over to my office in the jail, I wondered why so many gunmen were after me. The first thing I'd heard when I got back was about a couple of gunmen looking for me. I didn't see any reason to worry about them. It was still early in the morning. I let Joshua go get his breakfast at the hotel. He would bring a breakfast back to the only person in the jail. Buddy Farnsworth couldn't drink much, or he got mean. He couldn't back it up, so we put him in jail to keep him from being hurt. When Joshua returned, I told him, "I'm going over and have my breakfast and then you can do whatever you want to." Since he lived at the jail, he never had far to come to work.

I got back to the hotel and pushed open the door. The bell on the door signaled Susan that someone had come in. She peeped around the corner and waved at me. I sat down at one of the tables. Susan set a hot cup of coffee in front of me and went back into the kitchen. Madison set a plate of eggs, ham, and biscuits in front of me. We had the room full of people either eating or getting ready to. A young man sitting at a table a short distance from me had a buddy with him. He probably would not have gotten in trouble if he had been alone. He looked me over very carefully and said loud enough for everyone in the dining room to hear him, "You must know the lady who runs this place pretty well since you have my ham and eggs." The room got quiet. I ate my last bite of food and drank the last of my coffee. He said, "You might be a coward too." I pushed back from my table and took two quick steps toward him. He tried to get to his gun. I kicked him and his chair over backward. I spun on his buddy, and in one motion, I took his gun out of its holster. The cowboy lying on the floor made an effort to pick up his gun that had scooted away from him. I booted him in his face.

I scooped up his gun and stood there looking at both of them. I told them, "I don't normally give smart-aleck cowboys a second chance, but I figure you all are not real cowboys anyway." I called Susan out of the kitchen.

"Okay, boys, let's see how dumb you really are. You've got two choices. You can apologize to my wife, or you can go sit in my jail for a couple of months."

The one who started it told Susan, "I apologize, ma'am. I don't have much sense around beautiful women." His partner looked at me and said, "Thank you for not killing us. What is your name?"

I told him, "I'm Marshal Tom Davis. You are welcome in Santa Fe as long as you behave."

The cowboy who started the trouble said, "You are also Lone Eagle, the White Apache." He blanched, gulped, and said, "You ain't ever going to have any more trouble with us." He rubbed his jaw where I had kicked him.

I told them, "Breakfast is on me. Enjoy it." I left them with a little advice. "You are too young and way too slow to be tough smart alecks."

It was as if someone had opened the floodgates. Gunfighters came from everywhere. The smart ones looked me over and quietly rode away.

Most of them had been so close to death so many times that they had that sixth sense that told them they couldn't beat me fair and square. Wes Hardin, Jim Tighman, and Wyatt Earp had spread the word that if someone shot me in the back, they would personally settle with them. The rumor that gunfighters had a death wish was not true. They all planned to live a long life. Most of them didn't.

I got a telegram saying someone from Washington was coming to see me.

CHAPTER 19

Old Friends

I had a pleasant surprise a few days later. Captain Lin Miller and Top Sergeant Butch Gaston walked into the jail. After a period of talking of the last time I had seen them, Captain Miller told me, "We have a major problem on all of our Indian reservations. Sergeant Gaston and I were sent to inspect them. The reservations have short rations, and the meat they are given is almost rancid. They also have whiskey problems, even though whiskey is not supposed to be on reservations."

Captain Miller continued, saying, "We are mad at what we found. It seemed every one cheats the Indians. Corruption and the mistreatment of the Indians seemed to be rampant in most of the reservations. The president wants you to be the head of the Department of Indian Affairs with complete authority to do whatever you feel is necessary to protect the Indians. You would report to me, and I will make sure the information gets to the president. The president faces strong opposition in saving the Indians. I can authorize you to be the link between the Indians and the settlers since you are the only man who can listen to both sides and make a fair decision."

I knew Victorio would have wanted me to do it, so I agreed. But I had one exception: I would keep my job as marshal of Santa Fe.

Captain Miller said, "I can do better than that. I can swear you in as a federal marshal, representing the president." It could be bad soon. People with money were backing the ones who were trying to get rid of all the Indians. President Garfield was not well liked by everyone. Nor did he want to be.

They stayed a couple of days. Captain Miller was going to be made a colonel as soon as he got back in Washington. Sergeant Gaston refused a commission as a second lieutenant. I told Lieutenant Miller, "I have a new idea on how to make the reservations work. It will let them keep their pride. I have a new idea about all the Indians. Let them police and govern their own reservations. They will keep their word. They are harsher in their laws than we are. Let one of them from each reservation check the distribution of rations. Let them raise their own beef. Put me in charge of working with the Indians until it becomes what we want it to be. Indians will arrest Indians. A White Eye committing a crime in a reservation would be tried in an Indian court under Indian judges. It would take time but it would work. Indians committing crimes off the reservation will be tried in a settler's court."

Captain Miller thought it was a good idea and told Tom, "You will have to work this out. I'll tell the president that Sergeant Gaston, and I think it would be a good start toward peace between the Indians and the settlers." We came out with a few more ideas, and they had some also. When they left, we all knew at least the beginning of a new chance to save the Indians from being exterminated was in motion. It was a simple idea: let the Indians control the Indians. They would have their own jail and their own judge on the reservations. It would apply to the White Eyes. A settler would only work as an assistant in an Indian court. Captain Miller said that they would come back after discussing it with the president but to go ahead and begin the new system. I was now over all Indian reservations and over all the federal marshals.

I decided to send Susan and Caleb to a safe place. I told Caleb his job was to protect Susan if someone were to come after them.

I put on my Apache clothes and visited the reservations. I felt good about being able to live like an Apache for at least a few days. I ate beef jerky and a few rabbits. I also sampled the food given to the Indians. Not all of the rations given to the reservations were bad, but most of them were terrible. The Indians had nothing to do. That was half of the problem. The other half was that a lot of the Indian agents were crooks. We decided the next thing to do was to start an Indian school on each reservation. Upper Santa Fe was a lot quieter now and more prosperous. The town merchants on the wrong side of the tracks were beginning to wonder if I hadn't overstayed my welcome the last two years. Their business had suffered since I had been there. Some of the cattle drivers and mountain men passed Santa Fe by and went to Albuquerque or Taos, which were more open towns. No one seemed to remember how it had been when I'd first become marshal. You could have a quiet town or a rowdy one, not both of them. The only two not fussing were Jake, the owner of the livery stables, and McGregor, the owner of the mercantile store. The upper part of Santa Fe grew every day. Most of the big buyers of cattle used a letter of credit and did not have to worry about their money.

CHAPTER 20

Buck and Jerry

A couple of months after accepting my role as head of Indian Affairs, and while juggling my old and new responsibilities, I met two mountain men Santa Fe who were once friends with one another but, by now, had become sworn enemies. They both became my friends, only not at the same time.

It all had started over a simple misunderstanding. It had been Buck's time to check the traps. It had been about time to go down the mountain. The water in the streams had just about frozen solid. A few of the deeper places still had an occasional beaver, but they had to break the ice to set the traps.

Buck made his rounds pulling all the traps up so they could cache them for next season, if there was going to be a next season. Buck came to a part of the frozen stream that had a small drop to it. His feet shot out from under him. He landed on his back and zoomed down the frozen stream. He laughed at his own clumsiness and went back up the stream to where he had slipped. He started to go back to his traps when he thought of his fall and the fun he had zipping down the frozen stream. He took a short run and flopped down on the ice and went down it facedown. He was like a small child. He even laughed out loud. He slid down the stream until he got tired from walking back upstream.

He thought of Jerry and went up to get him so he, too, could slide down the stream. When he got back to the cabin, he thought it was strange there was no smoke coming from the chimney. He got his rifle ready and tried to open the door. It opened about a foot wide, enough for him to see Jerry lying against the door. He called out to Jerry, who didn't move at all. He cut the beaver straps that held the door in place and jerked the door off its frame. He started to check Jerry for any kind of wound when he smelled the booze. The last two-gallon jugs of whiskey were empty, and one of them was his. One was propped up upside down, and all the whiskey had drained out. Roger had drunk the other gallon and probably most of the one he had spilled.

Buck had saved his for the couple of days it took them to fix the cabin up for the winter and load their supplies. Buck was so mad he could have killed Jerry.

Supper was not cooked. The fire had gone out, and some small animal had gotten into their dry stuff, and sugar, flour, and meal were scattered everywhere. Losing his whiskey hurt the most.

Buck had gotten his horse and pack mule. He'd loaded half of the furs on it and left Jerry all the rest. He hadn't even written him a note. They had avoided each other from then on.

They had gone their separate ways, and every time they met, they didn't even look at each other. To speak would have started trouble. Every time they thought of it, they still got mad about it. It was the first time they were in Santa Fe at the same time.

Jesse Pirkle brought word to me that trouble was going to start in a few minutes in the Palace Saloon. Buck decided that this time he would settle the problem, and he was not going to back up an inch. Neither would Jerry. Buck, who got to Santa Fe before Jerry did, had been drinking for several hours.

The more he thought about, it the madder Buck got. Jerry had seen Buck, but he had ignored him. Jessie Pirkle beat me to the Palace and ran in the swinging doors. If two men had to fight and they didn't endanger others, I let them fight. Jessie was right. It might get out of hand since both men had friends with them. Buck was not drunk, but he had enough in him to make him mean.

Most of the old timers moved on down to Albuquerque, a more open town. The folks in Santa Fe would not mind if I got killed or retired.

In the mountains when they had a serious problem between two men, someone would ask, "Can you settle this without fighting?" Jessie asked the question just as I entered the Palace Saloon. I might have separated them, and they might have calmed down if Jessie had not been so eager to see them fight. I would remember his part in this. In the mountains, disputes were resolved with bowie knives. Most of the time, there were no winners. Both fighters got cut up pretty badly.

Buck was ready. It was time to end this. He slid his knife out of the scabbard and moved to the center of the room. Jerry did the same. I got there just in time. I motioned for them to put up their knives. Neither man paid any attention to me. I walked between them. I hit both of them in the head with my pistol. They were confused enough not to offer resistance. Jerry almost got to use his knife. Jessie and a couple of men at the bar helped carry them over to the jail. Jessie had egged them on, so I locked all three of them up in different cells. Sometime during the night, Buck and Jerry settled the differences between them. I let them out that morning. I kept Jessie in jail an extra day since he had helped make them fight by asking them if they were afraid of each other. They would likely never be partners again or even real good friends, but at least they were not enemies. They did become my friends who joined in my battle later on.

CHAPTER 21

Harry Cross:
A Real Gunman

A couple of days later, a real gunman came to town. It turned out he became the catalyst that brought the whole territory under fire. Ron Jedrokoski had disappeared. Ron had done much better than anyone realized. He owned a nice ranch not many people were aware of. It wasn't listed under his name. Not one of the five men who worked for him had ever heard of him or the name Jedrokoski. They wouldn't have been bothered by it though. He had two first-class gunmen. The rest carried scatterguns. It was hard to miss with a sawed-off shotgun. I'd had no news of him since I'd run him out of Phoenix. I knew he had been guilty of arranging all of the ambushes that had failed so far. I had been expecting some kind of action from him. Harry Cross was somewhat of a rarity in the gun-fighting business. I knew more about Harry than I did most other gunmen. We had been good friends for a couple of years. He always gave the other fellow a fair chance. He also was a family man. He had a ranch in Wyoming and almost had it paid for. He was a bounty hunter, but he always gave the ones he caught some money. In fact, some of the men who were wanted turned themselves in to Harry, and they got half of the money Harry got.

He stopped by the jail and came in to talk with me. As we sat drinking our coffee, he gave me something that made me understand what all this was about. It was what the gunmen knew that I didn't. He pulled a folded wanted poster out. It had my name on it. It also had a picture on it that didn't look like me. The poster said, "$1,000 reward for Tom Davis dead or alive." Harry wanted to quit the bounty-hunter trade, pay off his ranch, and stay home with his wife and three young children, two girls and a boy. This reward money would give him just enough money to pay the note on his ranch and buy a few cattle. He had told Ron, who had signed the wanted poster, he would take me on. Ron had signed it as Ron Jedrokoski, marshal of Prescott, Arizona.

I asked Harry, "Do you have to do this?"

He replied, "Yes, I do. I need the money."

I asked him, "You know Ron is wrong?"

He kind of shrugged his shoulders and slumped a little. He was not sure what he wanted to do now. He really needed the money. After thinking about it, he decided he had to take me on. He decided to have the gunfight after he finished his third cup of coffee. I could hear the wind getting up. I tried to talk him out of it.

I asked him, "What do you know about Jedrokoski? Can he pay for this?"

Harry said, "Ron owns six saloons and half of the red-light district in Prescott."

I told him, "Ron no longer owns any property. I do." I told him about the poker game and what I had done to Ron. Harry slumped a little more.

I told him that Ron could not be trusted and that he was the meanest man I had ever met.

I couldn't talk him out of the gunfight. He felt obligated to finish what he had promised. Ron had given him one hundred dollars in advance. We were about to go outside when the wind really picked up. We had waited too late. A dust storm came roaring up the street, covering everything in its path with dust. These storms could fill your lungs with sand in just a few minutes if you didn't have something to cover your nose and mouth. Harry took his pistol out and started cleaning it. I did too. Harry opened the door to go outside. A swirling circle of sand came dancing in the door.

I asked him again if he wanted to call it off since the blowing sand made it impossible to go on with the gunfight.

He thought about it for a few seconds and asked, "Do you think you really can beat me to the draw?"

I looked him straight in the eyes and told him, "Yes, I know I can. You have a wife and three children you are condemning to a terrible life if you fight me. I will certainly outdraw you if we have to fight, and I will surely kill you. Harry, do you really believe you can beat me to the draw?"

His face blanched, and he wore a stunned look.

Harry said, "I would be betting my life on it."

I told Harry, "If I have to kill you, I will send all of your belongings and a thousand dollars to your wife. It might last her a few months before she loses the ranch. Where will she go and what will she have to do to make a living?"

Harry looked at me again and said, "You really can beat me, can't you?"

I nodded my head and told him, "I have a business proposition for you. My partner has too many steers on the range we own. We want to expand, and from what you have told me, you have more grazing land than you need. We will pay you a thousand dollars to graze our steers on your land and for you to look after them. If you do a good job, we will pay you some more in longhorn cattle. You would have enough steers to have your own herd." Harry turned beet red as we shook hands sealing the agreement between us.

Harry looked at me and said again, "You really would have beaten me, wouldn't you?

I told him, "Yes, I can and I would have defeated you. Our ranch is about fifty miles from here. We will go to McGregor's and pick up some supplies, and we also need to go by the bank tomorrow to get your money. Keep up with your expenses, and we'll reimburse you. Randy Graham owns the bank. Cowboy will send some of his men to help you drive our steers to your ranch."

I offered him a room at the hotel we owned, telling him, "It's free this time, but next time we'll charge you, and you can give me a part of our money back unless your family comes with you. I'm sure my wife would be glad to meet them." The wind had quit blowing for a while. He decided to spend the night sleeping on one of the cots back in the cells. I slept on the one in the office.

I told Harry, "Go over to our hotel. Tell them I sent you. They will make you the best breakfast you ever had." Harry walked the few steps to the front door. He was so overwhelmed he couldn't say a word.

I said to him, "I'll see you later, and we'll take care of business." As he opened the door to step outside, I had a bad feeling wash over me. I hollered, "Don't open that door."

I was almost too late. He went for his gun and got it out just as two bullets thudded into the door beside him and one bullet hit him on his shoulder. I had my gun out and shot four or five times toward the sound of where the shots came from.

Harry realized he had been hit, and he might not make it. He motioned me over to him, and he had just enough time to say to me, "Please tell my family I love them." He passed out. He came to in a one of our hotel rooms with Doc standing over him. Doc even asked me for some of the Apache medicine, and after Harry got out of bed in two days, Doc put some in his medicine bag so he would always have some with him.

From now on, there would be no quarter asked and no quarter given. If we had to fight from now on, we would fight by my Apache rules. I was so mad I almost did something really dumb; I started to run out the front door. I got into the darkness of the shadow of the building next to where the shots had come from. I waited a few minutes, and then I moved closer to the building. I heard someone breathing hard. I told him to come out of the shadow where he was standing. A short man stepped out. He had blood running down his arm. Two men were dead. A wounded man was standing there. I put the wounded man in jail. His wound was not very bad. Doc could see him later.

The man asked me, "Are you going to let me bleed to death?"

I told him, "That's a good idea."

I was going to use him for bait.

I told him, "I'm going to let you go after you see Doc Jordan and have spent a couple of days in jail. That will give the one who hired you time to come down and kill you since you know too much. Ron is gone. Anyone working for him is now working free. I will get the ones who kill you. I will be waiting for them."

The little man told me everything since he would receive no money.

Harry was up and about in a week. He could ride his horse in four days if he wanted to go home. He surely did. It was time for me to run down Ron Jedrokoski.

CHAPTER 22

An Old Enemy

The Comanche, all but a few renegades, came back to their reservation. Old White Face (winter) beat them this time, not the White Eyes.

The beginning of a crazy couple of weeks was not too noticeable at first. A few gunmen rode into town and kind of looked me over. I knew what was going on, but since the first ones looked me over and had the instincts gunmen had about other gunmen, they moved on. They knew even if they were as fast as I was, they would still be killed. The odds were not so good.

A young kid came looking for me who didn't worry about the odds. He had to try me out. I broke his right shoulder. He was right handed. It wounded him up as a gunman and probably saved his life.

They kept coming. It was getting serious now.

Wes Harden, who had the reputation of being one of the fastest guns anywhere, stopped by the jail to see me.

He said to me, "I wanted to see a man who was worth one thousand dollars dead. Someone must want you pretty bad." I offered him a cup of coffee from the pot that never ran dry. He accepted it as most people did. No one ever turned down a cup of coffee. I wanted to ask him to explain what he had said, although I knew. He seemed to enjoy the coffee saying, "I don't get many times that I can relax and drink a cup of coffee in peace. Someone is always trying to get behind me."

"What did you mean by the one thousand dollars on me?"

"You have a reward on your head, and the amount of money involved is big enough to attract everyone, including me. You have wanted posters out on you in Arizona, Colorado, Texas, and New Mexico. Here's one of them." He brought out a poster that had been looked at a lot. It had wrinkles all over it. It had my name on it with the amount of the reward. It didn't look like me. It was signed Ron Jedrokoski, marshal of Prescott Arizona.

Wes held out his cup, and I filled it up again. "Why are you telling me this?"

"I don't feel good about this, so I decided to check you out. What does he have against you?"

I told him about the beating I'd given Ron and some of the facts about how mean he was. Wes had been in a saloon in Prescott owned by Ron.

Wes told me, "It seems Ron owns six saloons and a lot of the Red Light district. Ron has invented a new kind of poker. He doesn't show his cards. He just tells them what he has. It's a kind of poker where Ron decides which pots he wants.

"It seems it works as long as he has his gunmen around him. The previous owners were forced to play, and it seemed like Ron always won. He just told them that he had them beat with the hand he said he had. The only one who challenged Ron got a broken back out of it. That's pretty high stakes to play for."

He also owned or controlled the red-light district. He had the money and could pay the reward. Wes had his doubts about anyone living to collect the reward. Wes finished his fifth cup of coffee and stood up to go.

"Wes, when did you want to take me on?"

"Never," he said. "I was right about you. I don't know whether I am faster than you, but I have never killed anyone unless they needed killing. In fact, if you need my help, I would be glad to stay here a while until you resolve this."

I hired him as my chief deputy. It might have been one of my smartest moves.

Wes Harden shortened the odds considerably. No one in his right mind would want to take him on. Just the fact that he was my deputy ran a lot of wannabe gunslingers off. The real gunfighters didn't bother trying.

It had been a long time coming. I knew eventually Ron would see me again. It wouldn't be face to face. This time it would be an ambush or a hired killer. He had just declared war with me. There would be no mercy offered and no mercy given. I reverted back to being an Apache. This would be just like the war the Apache had fought their entire lives. I wired the marshal of St. Louis and told him to be on the lookout for Caleb's parents. His parents came in to see the marshal the next day. Some hunter had come upon the remains of his uncle (not very much of him left) and found some papers in the part of the charred Conestoga that hadn't burned. He let the marshal know about it.

I decided to send Susan to Virginia to stay with her mother for a few months. Mary, her mother, had two sisters who lived in Virginia. They were all widows.

After about a week, I received a telegram from Susan telling me Caleb's parents were in St. Louis and were going on to California. Caleb was now with his parents, much to everyone's relief. Susan continued on to Richmond, Virginia, to be with her mother and her sisters.

I called all my friends together who had asked to be part of cleaning up Phoenix and helping get rid of the several gangs of outlaws in the territory. I knew too many would take away the element of surprise. I settled on fifty of them. Almost everyone wanted to come.

I had Jerry and Buck, Wes Grafton, Tim Dukes, Cowboy, Wes Harden, Ramon, Don Luis Montoya, Joshua, Nana, Pete, Andrew, Mike, Nate, and Dad. I would add Gus and ten German miners to help me later on.

Ron could have as many as one hundred men, none of them first class. It could be interesting though.

CHAPTER 23

Let the Games Begin

My plan was to grow a beard and wear dirty clothes and miner's boots. I spent two weeks growing a beard and staying with my parents and Beth, my sister. Nate came over with his beautiful wife, and we caught up some things we had not talked about.

Dad told us about being a captain in the Confederate army. He had been very lucky to survive. During the conversation, they suggested that I become part of the mining crowd in Phoenix. My picture on the wanted poster didn't look like me, so I should be reasonably safe. I had a rider stop by and tell me Santa Fe was quiet. I had Neal Street, Joel Baily, Randy Gattan, Tim, Brian Street, and some other pretty good guns in Santa Fe to protect the town and the people. I would take Wes Harden with me. Joshua Gunter would come with us and be our messenger when the time came to clean out Phoenix. My authority from the president gave me authority over any law enforcement agency in the entire country. I was looking forward to confronting Ron Jedrokoski again.

I had a good trip to Prescott. Nothing unusual happened, much to my surprise. The first thing I did was get a job working and staying around some Germans miners who had come west to find their riches in gold and silver. Almost all of them were good, hard-working miners. I worked for a small amount of pay until I caught on and started working like the Germans. They worked smarter, safer, and produced more. Two or three of them decided if a mine was safe. If they said it was not safe, no German or anyone who knew them, like me, would ever work in it. I learned more and more. Best of all, they began to trust me. The German miners wouldn't work in a mine alongside a dangerous or forgetful man. The dangerous worker can work up top, but even then, someone keeps his eye on him. They would quit before they would take a chance on him. I learned a lot of whole sentences in German from them. After a couple of weeks, I let it be known that I was interested in buying a mine. It didn't take long for me to be approached by a miner who had not found enough ore to buy his food. I carried a couple of German miners over to look at the mine with me. The miner was leaving it in a mess, but it could be cleaned out and braced up. The miner was selling it cheap. Both of the German miners wanted to come to work for me. They told me that gold should be found in a couple of days if they worked hard at it. I agreed to take them on if their boss would let them go without any hard feelings. The foreman of Kimble Mining Company was glad to let them go saying, "I have to let two more go. We have not had a good strike in weeks." I hired the two extra miners. The man I bought the mine from had not eaten too well in that high-price mine area. He wanted to go back to California where he thought the grass was greener, although it never was.

I hired Wes and Joshua to work in the mine with the Germans and me.

They had to prove themselves also. The first thing we did was to make the mine safe. We shored up the top and sides of it and cleaned out the debris. The last miner had left it in a mess. Now it was clean and safe. We might have to abandon the mine in a hurry. We didn't want to fall over any trash. Trash also brought the rats, who were as big as cats. As luck would have it, on the seventh day, we struck a big vein of gold with traces of silver. The Germans were right. We took it to the assayer, and it proved out to be a good strike. The word got around.

One evening after I had been there about three weeks, I stopped in a saloon to see if Ron Jedrokoski was there and if he recognized me. The saloon was called the Naughty Lady. Some naughty ladies worked in the saloon. Most of them wound up with more money than the miners did. I knew this was one of the six saloons Ron had won without showing his cards. The original owners were long gone. Wes and Joshua stayed back to guard the mine since we had a good claim and claim jumpers were active.

I went to the end of the bar as usual, got my root beer. It was made from boiling sassafras roots in sugar water. Not everyone liked it. You had to develop a taste for it. Ron had a poker game going. He evidently didn't need to cheat this time.

He looked over at the bar and saw me. He had heard about my gold strike. He nodded at me, and I nodded back.

For a fleeting second, Ron thought, *something about that man is familiar.*

The man next to me was a German.

I asked him in almost perfect German, "Have you had any luck mining?"

He shook his head and said, "I have had no luck at all. I will have to find someone who needs a worker to help him." I told him to come out to my mine the next morning. I could use him.

Ron heard part of the conversation, and since it was in German, he forgot all about me.

He wasn't a very good poker player. I limped out of the saloon. Watching me go out the door, Ron thought, *I'll give him a few weeks to accumulate some money, and I'll get him in a poker game to take his money and his mine.*

Gustav Hienrich, the old German miner who had talked to me at the bar, proved invaluable. He loved America so much that he took an American name. He was now known as Gus Hambrick. He showed us how to clean the ore quicker. He also knew how to use dynamite. The vein of gold stayed good, and I was making a lot of money.

After thinking it over, I made what turned out to be one of my better decisions. I made all of them partners to share equally in the profit of the mine. More gold was being mined than before.

I continued going into the bar each evening and watching the poker games. There was only one player who played a respectable game of poker. Lonnie Taylor had grown up playing poker with his dad, who worked for the railroad. He might have a sixth sense also.

Ron kept watching me. There was something about me standing at the end of the bar and watching the poker games that disturbed him. That's why I was there. I started playing at the small-stakes table. I played bad deliberately but won anyway.

These feeder games were games where the winners eventually got a shot at one of the high-stakes tables. They were skinned at the big tables quickly. Lonnie Taylor was watching me also. He was playing at the high-stakes table where Jedrokoski played. Ron, for some reason (probably the name), had taken a liking for Lonnie and might hire him.

I played to win only a little money at a time so I would not draw attention to myself.

I had been coming in a few days when the real Ron Jedrokoski showed up. Ron was already mad at a cowboy who had won at his table and slipped out with the money. Jess Twillet happened to be playing a little later when Ron didn't show his cards. Jess was new in town and didn't know any better. When Jess turned Ron's cards over to see them, Ron knocked him over the table. Jess was hurt pretty badly from the unexpected blow. Jess wasn't dead, so Ron was preparing to stomp him. I kind of slid over until I had Ron blocked from Jess.

Ron said, "I caught him cheating. Anybody have any objections?" I motioned for two of my German miners to get Jess out of there. Jess had knocked over the table when Ron had hit him, and Ron's money was all over the floor. Ron lost some of it, but most of the people were afraid to get much of it.

No one got much. Lonnie Taylor dropped a couple of hundred and got out of the game.

CHAPTER 24

Phoenix, Arizona

I knew Lonnie Taylor was a good man who was wise enough to know when to get out. I stepped outside and stopped him. Lonnie pulled his pistol up in his holster to keep it from sticking. All gunmen did this. I asked Lonnie if he would like a job working with me.

Lonnie asked, "Why did you pick me?"

I told him I would tell him, but I would like to talk to him out at the mine first. Lonnie agreed to come, but he still had some doubts. He came out the next day and listened to the story of Ron and me. All the others backed my story. Lonnie was offered a share of the mine if he would work as general manager and deputy. All the partners agreed.

Business continued as usual. All of my men, except a couple of the men who usually played in the game, quit playing. They knew Jedrokoski was about ready to blow his top. Lonnie didn't like Jedrokoski.

He told me, "It sounds good. Let me think about it."

The next day, I left the saloon and walked down to the livery stable where he kept his horse. I waited for him to show up. Lonnie still wasn't totally sure about me. I let him read the letter from the president making me over every local lawman. I also told him I was Lone Eagle, the White Apache. He was stunned. Everyone had heard my story. He took a long look at me. After a few minutes, he agreed to ride out to our mine with me and join with us.

We rode out to the mine. Lonnie recognized Gus and a couple more of the men. He relaxed a little. He listened to me, and I showed the others the letter that said I was appointed as special marshal with total powers granted by the president of the United States. Lonnie joined up with us. It made a lot of sense. Counting my partners in the mine and the people coming from Santa Fe, I felt like I had enough men. I knew Ron Jedrokoski had to be stopped soon or a lot more men would be killed. I had found out all I needed to know. I deputized all of them as my men.

Joshua and Wes went back to Santa Fe to get their friends who were waiting for them. It should take them three or four days to get to Santa Fe and back. I told them to drift in one or two at a time and to stay out of the Perfect Hand Saloon.

As luck would have it, the fighting started sooner than I wanted it to, but we were ready for it.

I was standing in my normal place at the end of the bar when Ron motioned for me to come on over. He wanted a good look at me. I almost didn't go but changed my mind. My clothes were dirty; my face was covered with grime. I said a few words in German I had learned from Gus. I called Ron a dirty pig.

Ron relaxed. I wasn't anyone he knew. He motioned me to take one of the empty chairs at his table.

I shook my head and said, "I have no money on me."

Ron motioned me away and said, "Bring some with you next time." It was almost too early to take all of Ron's men on even terms, although he had a lot of bums and incompetent men in his gang. My guess would be about forty or fifty of them.

My friends from Santa Fe arrived, and they came in by themselves or with one other man. I deputized all of them. Prescott didn't know they had a legal marshal now. I made a list of the ones I would keep if they wanted to continue being deputies and the ones I would fire and/or put in jail. The miners were not afraid of Ron. They just wanted an even chance to get their hands on the outlaws. They were not gunmen.

I knew we might have to take on Ron and his men right away. Gus had a lot of miner friends who would like to get even with Ron. Ron had killed two of the miners and then made fun of the rest of them. Ron, since he was the town marshal, could get away with anything. He thought the entire town was afraid of him. They were waiting for the right moment and the right man. They hoped this was the right time and that I was the right man.

I was there the next evening. I had washed my face a little bit. Ron was not there. He had ridden out to our mine with some of his gunmen. Gus was there with some of his friends. Ron blustered and threatened and then backed down. It was too bad Ron backed down. He and I both sensed Gus was as strong and as tough as he was.

Ron thought, "Someone will have to shoot Gus in the back."

I sat and watched the game for a while. Ron came in and started his own game. It was almost honest. He had four captive poker players. All of them were afraid to leave. One of the men got up and left. Two others followed him. Ron motioned me over. I took my time getting over there, and I saw him tense up.

I had a note from the assayer saying that he had sent $3,000 over to the bank for me, and I gave Gus a note telling the banker to bring me the money. Gus kept the banker in his sights to make sure the money was safe. The banker had two of his men with him. Gus came in the saloon right behind the banker.

I told Ron, "Grown men play for real money. Which one are you?"

Ron jerked his head back, flushed, and said, "You'll find out in a few minutes." No one had ever talked to him that way. He had a fleeting thought that I seemed too sure of myself.

He shrugged his shoulders and said, "I'll take care of you before we are through today."

He still hesitated until I asked him, "Do you need someone to make your decision for you?"

A nagging fear ran through Ron as he thought to himself, "Who is this man?"

He debated for a few more seconds until someone started laughing at him. Everyone joined in the laughter. He decided he had nothing to lose since he would win by not showing his cards. We played for a few hours. I knew his card game already. He laughed when he had a good hand and frowned when he had a poor hand. He also had a card shark feeding him cards. Don Wilborne was a good poker player.

Ron played exactly like his personality. He was a smasher. When he was mad, he smashed something or somebody. It was almost time to show who I was to Ron Jedrokoski.

I played steady poker and got into Ron's pockets for about $500. I sent my money back to the bank when Ron ended the game by throwing the cards at one of his men.

I told Ron, "We will play again when you grow up." The laughter broke out again. He almost lost it all and would have if he had called me out. He knew I could beat him to my gun way before he got his out. He wanted to ambush me, but rumors of the gunmen in my employment scared him. Lonnie, Wes Harden, and I were at least even with his gunman, Bert Travis.

Bert Travis was thought to be the fastest gun in the West. That made two of them since Tim Dukes was also known as one of them. Throw in Wes Harden, and you had at least three fastest guns in the West. There was no doubt about it with some of the men. I was the only exception, and everyone but my men thought my name was Eric Strozier. Bert was also one of the men who still had his honor. It was a mystery why he stayed with Ron.

CHAPTER 25

The War

Bert was also a man who reasoned things out. He went his own way no matter what the odds were. Looking at Ron, he had the feeling he was backing the wrong man.

Ron thought to himself, "Bert can handle Eric Strorich all right."

Bert was a rarity—an honest, dependable man who had kept his independence since everyone was afraid of him. They were right; they should be.

Ron really did not like Bert because Bert got all the attention. Bert didn't like Ron either and didn't care if Ron knew it.

Ron thought, "After this job is over, I will settle with Bert my own way."

Bert knew something was not right about Ron. He didn't like or trust him. He would have to watch his back. He had almost enough of Ron. He knew he needed someone to cover his back now.

Bert also knew the man at the end of the bar was big trouble, and after a couple of evenings watching me, he knew it was Ron that I was pursuing. Ron would not take me on by himself. He also knew it would be hard to beat me in a fair fight, so he decided to talk to me and hear my side of the story.

I got $1,500 in gold changed to poker chips. I counted the poker chips and found them to be thirty dollars short. I grabbed the man who had shorted me and turned him upside down. I picked up my thirty dollars from the money dropped on the floor. Ron looked the man over. He started to say something to me about the thirty dollars. He changed his mind. He knew the man had been stealing under his orders. The man probably had been stealing some of Ron's own money also. The man disappeared. He didn't stop to pick up any of the money on the floor. In a few seconds, the money on the floor disappeared.

I looked Ron square in the eyes as I sat down at the table with him. At first, both of us played cautiously, and I gave away a couple of hands to see how Ron reacted. He was pretty obvious. It looked like it was my time to let Ron know who I was. I was about to call his hand.

I switched the deck to one just like it. Now they couldn't read the backs of the cards. I had already put three queens on the top of the new deck. When I picked up the cards to give to Sawyer to deal, I palmed the three queens. Sawyer knew some cards were missing. He could feel the difference in the weight of the deck. He thought Ron had them. Sawyer gave Ron his pair of tens off the bottom. The signals went out that this was the hand in which they would take my money. They needed to be ready for trouble. Several of his men changed positions. My men changed with them. As it sometimes happened, you got lucky. I drew two cards. I drew my fourth queen and a five. Ron drew a pair of kings. He had two pairs, tens and kings. Ron bet $6,000 on his hand. I raised him $4,000. I liked to keep the money even. The dealer nodded at Ron who raised another $5,000. I called. One of the crooks signaled something to Sawyer. Nate led him out of the saloon. In a minute, you could hear him leaving town. Nate came back in. He moved almost behind me. He had my back covered. I nodded at Wes Harden. He had got back in town a couple of hours ago. The other men from Santa Fe were in town also. Some were in the saloon. Wes walked by the man standing on my right, leaned over, and whispered to him, saying, "You probable ought to go stand by the front door because I'm going to put a bullet in the space you're standing in now. In fact, I think you had better go outside and get on your horse, leave, and never come back. Give me your gun and leave. You have fifteen seconds." The man started to balk at this until he looked into Wes's eyes and saw death there. Gus was sitting at the bar, having a good time watching this. He had picked out two goons who were enforcers for Ron. He would handle them.

Ron had not followed any of this. He was so caught up in his thoughts of winning all of the money that he missed everything going on. Something about me still disturbed him. This German miner resembled the man that he vaguely remembered beating him up so badly. It had taken him months to recuperate. He had never been afraid of anyone before, but he was having a hard time sleeping. He hated me so much he wanted to kill everyone in my family. He had kept up with me and my family and friends. He knew he was still afraid of me. The reward for each of my family members ought to do the job. He had a lot more money than that. He bought a lot of men who had no principles.

He brought his attention back to the poker game. Sawyer gave Ron his third ten, giving him a full house. He had three tens and two kings. It didn't matter since he was not going to show his cards anyway.

Ron forced himself to pay attention to the game. Ron gave the signal to his goons to get ready. They got off the barstools and ambled over to the table. They didn't see Gus walking right behind them. Ron bet a thousand. I bumped him a thousand.

Ron told me, "Let's play some real poker."

He made a motion to Sawyer, who threw in his cards. Now it was just Ron and me.

Ron knew he was going to win. He had the advantage. He laid his cards on the table face down.

"What do you have in mind?" Ron kind of grinned. "You have a good gold mine claim, and I have six saloons. I will bet my saloons and all their money against your gold mine."

I responded, "Are you sure you want to do this?"

Ron sneered. "What are you afraid of?"

I told Ron, "I want to see proof that you own those saloons. I don't trust you." Ron's face flushed beet red. He told the bartender to get the banker and his deeds.

"Tell Mr. Morton to give you my deed also," I said. Ron glared at me the entire ten minutes it took Mr. Morton to bring the deeds. When the banker got there, I told him to hold the deeds and turn our cards over one at a time and give the deeds to the winner.

I told him, "Start with Ron's." The banker turned each card slowly. Ron started to protest, but he wasn't worried. He had the cards. The first card was a ten. Ron shrugged. The second card was a ten. Ron smiled. The third card was a king. The fourth car was a ten. The banker turned Ron's last card. It was a king. Ron had three tens and a pair of kings—a full house. Three tens would win 90 percent of most hands. Mr. Morton turned my first card over. I had a queen. My second card was a five of diamonds; I couldn't have a straight flush or a royal flush.

The banker turned over another card. It was a queen. The next card was a queen. I was showing three queens with a five of diamonds. Only one card in the entire deck could beat Ron's full house.

If the banker turned any card but a queen, Ron would own our mine. The banker picked up my last card and held it facedown for a few seconds. Ron started to squirm, and he was sweating enough to wet his pants from it. His face turned beet red. The banker flipped the card over on top of the rest of my cards. It was a queen. My partners in the gold mine and I owned six saloons.

Ron was speechless. He started to stand up, snatching for his gun. My pistol pointing at his gut kept him in his seat. The two goons started to come around the table to grab me. Gus grabbed each of them by the front of their shirts, picked them up, and slammed their heads together. One of them couldn't get up, and the other one wouldn't. Gus reached down picked the goon up and hit him in the face. Now the second goon couldn't get up. Gus looked around to see if anyone else wanted to help Ron. No one volunteered. Ron went ghostly white. He knew who I was and what I was about to do.

CHAPTER 26

Cleaning Up Phoenix

Ron had an ace in the hole, or he thought he did. He had a man standing at the bar in case he lost. He was supposed to shoot me. Wes Harden shot the man as he raised his gun. He had already picked the man out. He didn't kill him, but he would have trouble forever.

The worse blow of all to Ron was Bert Travis, who he had depended on so much. Bert hit the bartender on his head with his pistol.

Bert turned to Ron and said, "I don't like crooks, cowards, or bullies, and you are all of these, along with being a four flusher." Bert asked me, "Can you use some help?" I nodded my head. The banker gave me the deeds.

I told the crowd, "Free drinks for one hour." Ron blanched and started to grab me. He had a flashback. Ron shuddered as his memory returned.

All of this seemed to have happened to him before.

It had to be me. Ron's thoughts went back to his recovery and his pledge that he would destroy me one day. He was filled with a terrible fear that I would whip him right now and humiliate him again. He was trembling all over. His fury almost got him killed, and he knew it. He thought he had overcome his fear of me because he had more or less made a success of himself, and most people were afraid of him. He had built a fortune, and he still had most of it—at least he thought he did. The six saloons and the red-light district brought in unbelievable amounts of money. He had lost the saloons and everything that was part of them, like their checking accounts.

Mr. Morton told me, "Tom, you have an enormous amount of money in the names of the saloons your partnership has won."

Ron knew he would always be afraid of me. He knew he could not whip me. He could not beat me in a gunfight. The only solution was to pay someone to kill me. He no longer had the money to do that. If he had the money, he would continue. He would have it done whatever the cost. That was the reason for the reward of $1,000 on me. The reward was no longer good, so the posters were taken down. He stood up. I grabbed him by his arm and belt and ran him out the door. He flew through the air and landed on his face in the street. He got up and half ran, half staggered toward the stable. Someone pushed him, and he lost his balance and fell down again. The laughter of the crowd followed him down the street and over to the livery stable, where he got his horse and started to ride slowly out of town with his head down. I stopped him and tore the marshal's badge off his vest.

I said to him, "By the power invested in me by the president of the United States, I am taking your badge and taking a warrant out on you. You will never have a moment the rest of your life where someone will not be after you." He never looked me in the eye. His hatred for me was so great, he could think of nothing else except killing my family and me.

I told him, "At ten in the morning, a reward of two thousand dollars will be posted all over Phoenix, and then all over this territory, to anyone bringing you to the Phoenix jail, where Wes Harden is now marshal. The reward will be paid out of your money. Mr. Morton astounded us by telling us that since we owned the saloons, all the money in the other banks listed under the name of the saloon or Ron went with them. We had struck it rich again. I told Ron. I hope you live long enough to serve a lifetime jail sentence. The hunt for you begins tomorrow."

I let Ron go, slapped his horse on its rump, and watched it run out of town. Ron was in a hurry now.

CHAPTER 27

The Hunted

I gave Mr. Morton a list of my partners. I told him to divide the money evenly, as the partnership included every man working with me, including the marshals, the miners, and the ranch workers. The marshals entered every saloon, every house of ill repute, and every gambling pit and rounded up every one of the outlaws. I sent Wes, Joshua, and four others over to the saloons to make sure no one got the money in the boxes kept under the counter. They were taking advantage of the free whiskey. I asked the banker to get me six honest men. The banker came back with them in about twenty-five minutes. I asked them if they wanted to run a saloon and be a partner with me and the miners. All of them were quick to agree. I told them to fire all of the old bartenders and take the cash over to the bank. Starting tonight, each of them owned half of a saloon.

Mr. Morton told the banker, "Keep an eye on the flow of money from the saloons and keep the money coming from each saloon separate. If there are any changes in the revenue, let me know." The town went crazy- in a good kind of way! I was a hero. Whiskey flowed freely. Everyone was happy except Ron and the few men he had left. He was already trying to figure out how to kill me.

Ron was now a marked man. His solitary ride out of town cost him his reputation. He was fair game now. His great strength was of no use to him. Someone was going to collect the $2,000 on him, probably real soon if he was not careful.

Ron left Phoenix that night. He thought about burning down two of the saloons, but he was afraid I would catch him. I had let him go to humiliate him. I had succeeded. He had no confidence now. I planned to put him in jail for the rest of his life.

One quiet, uneventful week had passed and it was time to go after Ron. He sent me word that he would kill me and every member of my family. I hoped to take him alive so that he could remember my family and me every day when he woke up in prison, looking for a way to survive the day. Susan was safe. Mom and Dad, Nate, and Cowboy were safe too. Nana was keeping an eye on them at my request.

I asked Wes Harden to be the marshal of Prescott until I could get a new one. I knew Nana would keep my dad and the family totally safe.

I met with Nana and deputized him. It was the only time an Apache looked out for settlers and was going to arrest a former marshal if he saw him. Perhaps fifty or sixty outlaws were still in the territory near Phoenix. I was going to leave them to Wes and the marshals, and I was going after Ron. I didn't want any help. Everything changed.

A shot rang out. A geyser of sand appeared beside me. It seemed that it was not over yet between the outlaws and me. Several more bullets kicked up sand. I spurred Sugar Foot in the side with my soft spurs, and we took off. Someone had gotten too eager or they might have gotten me. In a few minutes, I was out of bullet range. They stayed behind me. I liked that.

It was total war now. Chances were these men didn't know about Phoenix being cleaned up, or about Ron on the run with no money to pay them, or no more free booze. The cloud of dust thrown up by the horses stained the yellow sky to the southwest and southeast of me. The amount of dust told me it was not a sizable group, maybe twenty men. They were the last of Ron's outlaws. A shot rang off to the southeast. It told me the two groups of men a short distance behind me were working together. Ron must have had a lot of money to hire that many men. They were funneling me to the lower range of the Sandia Mountains. If they could make me stay on this line, I would be facing more than twenty men if I was right about the amount of dust rising on both sides of me. If I had to continue into the mountains, more men might be waiting for me. I might still have about a half an hour before they made contact with me.

My sixth sense was strangely quiet. I knew it would come soon. Right now, I had to depend on myself entirely. It was not a bad feeling. I had not pushed Sugar Foot, my horse, at all. The men surrounding me were in no hurry. They had me boxed in, and they knew it. Their plan had one weakness. There was one possibility, and it was dangerous. It had never been done before. No one with good sense would try it. Sugar Foot was maybe the only horse that could do it. A mile further on was a canyon that had a steep drop-off from the top to the bottom.

If I could get halfway down it on the slope that was not as steep and slide over ten feet to the right as we went down, we could get onto the slope's other half that was even less steep. I could really surprise them later on.

My side of the canyon had a gradual slope that turned into a hundred-foot drop straight down. If we hit that slope, I would have no chance at all. The only possible way to get down from there was your horse must be able to slide ten feet right on the more gradual slope before you got down to where the wall went straight down. This new slope was still steep, but I believed Sugar Foot could handle it.

Sugar Foot perked up when we got to the canyon. I knew hesitating would not help any, so I rode her right over the rim in the only place that was not steep as the rest of it. Sugar Foot spread her legs and sat down on her haunches to give her balance as we went over the rim. It looked impossible. I squeezed my knees to give her directions to move right. She had already done it.

Sugar Foot stayed with it. We had covered half the distance down to the drop-off and had moved right only a couple of feet. It didn't look like we were going to make it. That's when Sugar Foot took over. She spread her legs on her left side and pulled them up on her right side. By the time we got to the beginning of the drop-off, we had shifted the ten feet and more, and we hit the less steep slope. Sugar Foot had kept her balance all the way down. She shuddered to a stop as we reached the bottom.

The men on my trail had a couple of trackers with them. The sign was pretty clear that I had gone over the side. Ray Gander, who had some Apache blood in him, told Bob Foster, the leader, "If he can do it, so can I." He rode his horse over to the place I had gone over the side. He tried and tried to make his horse go over the side. Finally, the horse had enough. He started bucking, trying to get Ray out of the saddle. He was a whole lot smarter than Ray. The horse went over the rim of the canyon sideways. Being part Indian didn't stop Ray from screaming all the way down until he hit the bottom.

He didn't know that Ron and his money were gone. Everyone working for Ron now was now working without pay. It didn't matter at all to Ron.

CHAPTER 28

The Remaining Outlaws

I decided to give them something to think about.

I led Sugar Foot to their picket line. They had left one guard to stay with the horses. They never seemed to learn. One guard in Apache territory was asking for trouble. No one thought I might be on this side of the mountain. The guard was very tired. Besides that, he was eating. He took out his piece of bread and meat and took a bite of it. He set his canteen in front of him. I had my Apache gear on. I had knee-length boots, a breech-cloth, headband, and all of my fighting gear.

I covered half the distance before he turned around. He glanced at me and then took another bite of his sandwich and a swallow of water. The water had to be a little warm. It made you want to spit it out until you realized it was all you had and not much at that. The guard turned back to see the Sandia Mountains light up with the morning sun.

He thought he wanted to be the first to see me. He didn't. I walked right up to him. He had one moment to wonder who I was. He didn't know of anyone else who was coming. It dawned on him that I might be the one they were after. It was too late for him. By the time I got there, he was trying to get his knife out.

I had my bowie knife in my hand. Instead of killing him, I knocked him unconscious. I wanted to shake them up. I wrote the outlaws a note and put it in the unconscious outlaw's mouth. The note said, "I'm coming after all of you. You will need to get you some more men to help you. I have stolen all of your horses on this side of the mountain. I have all of your food and water. Tell the men who have to walk back not to buy any expensive horses. Buy some nice clothes. They will need the clothes to be buried in. I will get all of you sooner or later if the Apaches don't get you first."

I moved the horses slowly at first. Sugar Foot and I started back to find Nana, with Sugar Foot becoming the leader of the horses. Most of the outlaws were through. They would move on when they got back to Phoenix. I gave half the horses to the Comanche back at Fort Stanton and the other horses to the Apaches at Fort Apache. Sharing the horses encouraged the Comanche to come in with me.

It was my game now. Ron had wanted war, and now he had it. Don Luis joined us. I figured Ron had about fifty outlaws left, and they were mostly drifters and bums. He did have a few good gun hands left. Free whiskey had made some of them stay with him.

I sent their half of the horses to the Fort Apache Reservation and gave them to the few Apache still living there. They moved the horses to a secret place and then sold them.

I was safe. They didn't catch me this time, but I knew they would keep on trying. What they didn't know was I was going after them. I already had them spooked. Most of them would get out of the outlaw business. The canyon ended a couple of miles away, and I could cut across and go back to where the remaining outlaws would spend the night. Their campfire would lead me to them. It might be my father's ranch they would choose to raid if we left them alone. Nana would be there for Dad if he needed someone and if the outlaws came. I would find out what the outlaws planned or I would let them know they had made another big mistake. They didn't know it, but life had just turned bad for them. An Apache Indian would break off an attack if he felt Ussen was against him. Most of these men would die because of their stupidity. Ron was going to get a lot of them killed, and it didn't bother him.

One of Nana's warriors was just crossing their back trail. Nana had told them to watch out for men who traveled in a gang. It was the men who were on the southwest trail. He followed them until they stopped for the night and then he turned his horse toward Nana's village, a couple of hours away. Nana loved it. He was going to get to take some bad men out. This war was about to warm up.

I found them no more alert than the last outlaws. I slipped through the sleeping men.

I got Sugar Foot and circled around to the end of the picket line that held the horses.

The first light of the sun started to brighten the sky. A movement near the horses got my attention. I looked closer, and there was Nana, grinning at me. He had two warriors with him. He made sign that he wanted to handle this. I nodded my head in agreement and slowly walked Sugar Foot to the edge of the camp. It was hard to believe that over twenty outlaws were there and none of them woke up. The empty whiskey bottles around their campfire told the story.

Nana cut the picket line that the horses were tied to. The two Apaches had positions around the camp. All of them shouted the Apache war cry at the same time. I raised my rifle and shot over the men lying around the fire, sleeping. I emptied my Winchester all around them. The horses were already skittish because of Nana, Sugar Foot, and me. The Apache did the same, shooting their rifles into the air. The horses ran right over the men in their path. Some with their rifles tried to dodge the horses. Some of the twenty outlaws tried to put on their pants and boots while holding onto their guns. It was a disaster for them. Sugar Foot and I hazed the horses into the desert.

Only five men were unharmed. Many of them suffered broken bones. Only one was unlucky. He had his rifle pointed at Nana, who shot him. They were lucky that only two were badly injured. The outlaws were without horses and had only a little food and water until I came up with a good idea. We made all the outlaws give us their guns and take off their boots. I drove the outlaws' horses back to their camp and put them on their horses. We tied their hands behind them and let Sugar Foot and me lead the horses back to Santa Fe. Next came Nana and his two warriors, wearing their marshals' badges while they brought in the outlaws.

Most of the survivors got out of the outlaw business right then. They would find a better job. Five of them were separated from the rest. They had wanted posters on them.

One problem they had was their number, and we had cut that down already. It was their misfortune they bumped into Nana, some of his warriors, and me.

Ron only had a few men left, and most of them were leaving right away.

The Miracles at San Miguel

San Miguel was one of those towns started by accident. The Gonzales family was the only family that continued living there. It was after Coronado came through exploring the land for gold for Spain. Ten families had moved into it from Spain under land grants from King Phillip. The first family that moved in had been named Gonzales. All of the others had left with Cortez after a period of hardship.

After debating about how small it was, Coronado had decided to list it as a town on his maps. In the late 1700s, the Pima Indians had decided to run off the few Spanish who had drifted onto their land. It had been a mistake. A few hardy Spaniards with muskets, although outnumbered by the Pima, had fought fiercely against them. After a brief encounter, it had turned out the muskets won. The Pima had needed to move down into Mexico, and the town of San (Saint) Miguel had been listed as a mission town owned by Spain. Cortez had been ordered to put a small Catholic mission at San Miguel.

Hernando Cortez had cut the size of the one-room mission in half (to five hundred square feet.) He had put the Gonzales family in charge of it and left as quickly as he could. Tito's grandfather had inherited the mission church that had long been forgotten by

Spain. The Gonzales family living in the old mission had become part of the countryside, no longer citizens of Spain.

A priest had been assigned to it in the early 1800s. Pablo's father had been the priest's assistant. Pablo had become the official priest when his father and the priest had died. Even he considered himself to be a priest now.

Ron Jedrokoski rode slowly out of town, his mind all shook up. His mind was in a frenzy. I had humiliated him again. All he could think about was getting revenge. The story of Ron's humiliation had been told over and over. Many of the gunmen had decided California was a good place to visit. So were Atlanta, Chicago, and New York.

My marshals had all been in place. All of them had been assigned a place to be in when I took Ron down. At about ten o'clock, I had won all of Ron's saloons and his red-light property. Ron had been thrown out into the street and ridden out of town a few minutes after ten. The rats had begun leaving the sinking ship right behind him. All of them had funneled through the marshal's office. Wes had been ready. Notices had been put up saying the outlaws had amnesty until noon the next day.

The marshals had appeared at their appointed places. They had been everywhere. They had their badges on. A ripple of shock and excitement had gone through every saloon, every house of ill repute, and every gambling joint in Phoenix. The outlaws had been surrounded and boxed in. Their guns had been taken from them. Only two of them had offered any resistance. A quick hit on their heads with a pistol had stopped that instantly.

A count had been made of the ones who had left early (twenty-three) and the ones given amnesty (seventeen). The number locked up (twenty-two) had been added to it, and a total of sixty-two outlaws had been counted. Ten who had been locked up were later strung up by the hanging judge.

Ron had gotten a spare horse and some money he had hidden there during his prosperous years and taken off for Nogales, Mexico. His money would make him a wealthy man in Nogales, for it would be a lot of money in Mexico. He might be able to hide and buy protection from the marshal, although he really didn't believe that. He knew I was coming after him. He wondered why I let him go in the first place. Then he understood: I wanted to chase him down, make him look over his shoulder every few minutes to see if I was there. He calmed down a little and finally accepted the fact that he had been real lucky. He could have, should have, been killed.

My marshals and I had cleaned up Phoenix. All of Ron's gunmen had been offered a second chance. Signs were posted all over town. The real merchants, the ones who helped build the town, were jubilant. I asked them to help me clean up Phoenix again. It was now a town of 5,245 people. It belonged to the citizens again. The rest of the outlaws could leave after going over to Marshal Wes Harden's office with the understanding that Yuma awaited those caught committing any crime anywhere. Most of them left town almost as soon as they cleared the jail.

I had one thing left to do: take Ron Jedrokoski out of circulation forever.

Ron was on the old road between Mercado and San Miguel known as the Old Mercado Boulevard. It followed the narrow, shallow Sabine Creek for several miles until the creek disappeared into the desert sands a few miles away. Without Sabine Creek, Mercado would not have existed.

Ron had the two bags full of money on his horse. He was going toward a town called San Miguel. It was really not a town. It was a one-room catholic mission built in 1537. It had its good and bad times. The Gonzales families had been part of its history for 150 years. It was ready for a miracle.

Pablo Gonzales was the only priest within a two-hundred-mile radius, and he wasn't a real priest. His great-grandfather had been the assistant to the priest. When the priest had passed away, the Gonzales men had continued on, and Pablo and his family had become a line of priests. Most of them couldn't read Spanish or English, much less Latin. They memorized enough to sound officious and get by. Tito Gonzales and his family lived in and took care of the mission that was almost surrounded by the red canyon walls that had at one time funneled the Sabine Creek through the canyon. The mission sat some 175 feet from the dry bed. It was on a ledge fifteen feet above the creek bed. Pablo came to the mission at least four times a year and loved coming.

Ron's head was still teeming with thoughts of revenge. He turned his head sharply at the yelping of some baby coyotes about one hundred yards from him. He wanted to make sure it was coyotes and not Indians.

A blinding light flashed through his head, and a great pain came from behind his eyes. He fell from his horse, landing on his back in the gravel. He held tightly to the horse's reins. It bucked and the extra horse jerked free. Ron landed on the back of his head, knocking a deep hole in it. He was briefly knocked unconscious. Although Ron's left side was half paralyzed, he was almost back on his feet and trying to get up on his horse when a second bolt of light and pain seared through his head. It knocked Ron to his knees and then on to his face. He held the reins to his horse in his right hand with a death grip. Ron's weight pulled the horse's head down slightly. It kept the horse from running away. It was a good thing since his horse had the pair of waterproof, leather saddlebags stuffed with over $10,000 in each of them on its back. If the horse had gotten free, he would have been a goldmine for whoever caught him.

Ron got halfway up before he fell and landed on his face again. The rocks again punctured and broke his jaw, nose, and cheekbones but missed his eyes.

Ron suffered two massive strokes and one small stroke. The light was gone from his mind. Major damage had been done to his brain, limiting his cognitive and motor skills. Though he was still living, Ron Jedrokoski did not exist anymore to anyone who knew him. All of the knowledge part of his brain, his past, and his speech were wiped clean. He was totally out of it. His meanness was also taken away by the strokes.

He kept a death grip on his reins. Blood made small rivers down his back and the side of his head, making a puddle on the ground. The blood finally clotted, and the flow ceased.

Ron had been knocked-out for five hours when a large two-wheel wagon drove up. It held Tito Gonzalez, his wife, Juanita, his teenage daughter, Mercy, and Ruiz, his eight-year-old son. The Gonzalez family was on their way back home to San Miguel from Mercado. They had done some necessary shopping. It was only twenty-one miles from the mission, but it had taken them two days. They had enjoyed the trip and looked forward to it. The figure in the road was so bloody and his face so disfigured it made them all want to throw up. Mercy started to cry.

Tito had to cut the reins to get them out of Ron's hand. He tied the horse to the back of his wagon after they got Ron into the wagon. It took all of them to do so, and even then, they almost dropped him. Ron didn't know but his brain had suffered two major traumas. He was lucky the clots had dissolved after the second stroke. Tito knew they were still six hours from their one-room mission. The man might not make it.

Nita soaked a rag in water and carefully wiped the blood off of Ron's wounds. He didn't even quiver. She forced tiny swallows of the water into his mouth.

Ron breathed in a high, rasping voice, trying to get air into his lungs. Nita knew something had to be done since his breathing was getting more labored.

Tito stopped the wagon, and he and Nita forced Ron's broken jaw open. The bone breaking in his jaw sounded like a gun going off. She found several broken teeth in his mouth. She got them out and left his jaw wide open. His breathing got better right away.

They got home, and Tito took Ron's saddlebags into the mission and threw them over into a corner full of old rags and clothes. Nita would pull the old cloth apart and use the threads again to make clothes for her family. Ron was put on a pallet made out of a couple of blankets and an old quilt put on the floor. He had not regained consciousness.

Tito got on Ron's horse and lit out for the midwife's rundown shack a few miles away. She was the closest thing to being a doctor out here. Trained by her mother and also being a midwife, she learned quickly. She felt she had been sent to the people around San Miguel by God. They felt the same way.

It took Tito four hours to get her and her supplies back to the mission. Tito had described Ron's condition to her, so she had brought a full bag of aloes and medicines.

Delores took one look at Ron, shook her head, and began what she first thought was going to be a losing fight.

Ron's horse was not overloaded with Tito, Delores, and the supplies. It didn't bother the horse much since she had carried Ron a long time, and Ron was as heavy as the two of them. He was much bigger and heavier than most men. The midwife's examination of him started at the top of his head. It bothered her that at no time did she see or feel him move when she examined him.

Pablo, the priest, arrived on one of his journeys about the same time that morning. Delores and Tito got to the mission with the medicines soon after the priest and midwife did. The Mendez family explained how they had found Ron and didn't know who he was. Pablo also thought Ron looked terrible and that his wounds were terminal. Pablo and Tito undressed Ron and put a nightgown on him. They were getting him ready for Pablo's final rites. No one in the room thought he would make it through the day, but Pablo spent two weeks with Ron, praying for him. He finally began to believe Ron had improved some and might make it. The first good sign was the amount of soup Ron began to drink. It had increased dramatically.

Pablo had to make his rounds, so he was gone for ten days. Ron had been unconscious for thirty-one days and had not moved or cried out many times.

The midwife started using the mission as her home base. She saw the old, bloody clothes laying on top of the bags at about the same time Pablo returned from Mercado. Nita and the midwife had the same idea at the same time. Maybe he had some clean clothes in the saddlebags.

Tito picked up one of the bags, opened it, and dumped the contents on the floor. It was money! It was a lot of money! They were all stunned. A grunting sound coming from Ron's pallet caught their attention. Everyone turned to look at Ron, who, for the first time, was trying to sit up. His eyes opened in alarm.

The deep cuts on his face had scabbed over, and scars had begun to appear in their places. He had lost over seventy pounds. His hair was solid white. The deep bruises on his face had gone from blue to black to deep purple. His jaw was out of alignment even though they had reset it. His nose was grotesque. The midwife had inserted hollow water reeds in his nostrils for several weeks, and this had helped keep the air passages opened. Even with all of his disfiguration, he was still a commanding figure.

Pablo gave him his new name when he said, "He is a magnificent gringo, El Grande Gringo."

The Miracle of San Miguel had begun. Pablo traded a Texas cowboy Ron's horse for the Texan's horse and thirty dollars. The

Texan was on his way home and needed a good horse. It was a good trade on both sides. They needed the money to buy food.

Ron felt strange. He didn't know who he was or where he was. He didn't know any of the people around him. He knew he was at total peace with himself for the first time in his life. His left side was stiff, and when he tried to talk, his speech came out garbled. Everyone looked at him and then at the money on the floor.

Pablo asked El Gringo, "Is this your money?" El Gringo moved his head, and it looked like he was answering yes. "Did you want to give some of it to the Mission?" It looked like he nodded yes again.

"Would you like to stay here until you are able to leave?" Tito asked him. "Are we to use the money to pay for you staying here?" A sense of goodness seemed to illuminate El Grande.

Pablo asked the others, "Did he just give us the money if we let him stay here?" El Grande seemed to be nodding yes again. Pablo asked each of them. "What is he telling us?" All of them thought El Grande Gringo had given them the money to use on the mission just like Pablo said.

It was a good bargain for him because he had a place to stay the rest of his life if it was necessary.

In truth, he could not control his motions. He was paralyzed on his left side. He tried to sit up again before he slid back into the deep sleep again. He didn't make it.

Pablo prayed and considered the money a gift from God. The Mendez family agreed with Pablo. So did Delores. They would ask Ron again later on and do what he said. If he wanted them to, they would repair and add on to the mission.

They waited two days until Ron (now El Grande Gringo) seemed to be more clearheaded. He gained his strength rapidly, although he would drag his left foot forever, and his left arm would always be stiff and undependable. His words were not clear but when Pablo asked Ron if he wanted the money to be spent on the mission, they got a nod they all thought was a clear yes. El Grande Gringo" would have a place to stay forever.

The first building project was a room for El Grande. The room was twenty-five by twenty feet. It would be called a big room by any standard. It had a dresser, chairs, a large bed, bedside table, and a private bath. Windows with shutters gave him a view of the sky. He improved every day.

After a month, he had his room. A family of adobe brick builders moved into town and opened a business, making adobe bricks for the new room and homes for new settlers. The work on the mission kept them busy all the time. Water was now available to everyone. The Sabine Creek was now called the Gila River. It was a river with a good flow. It had been running full since the night of the big storm over three weeks ago. Tito had thought they were going to lose the mission for a few minutes when the rising waters made it an island for a short period of time.

Ten thousand years ago, the Gila River had run full and strong. It had cut a path through the Red Rock Canyon to allow the river to run through. It had taken almost all of ten thousand years for the river to finish cutting a path in the canyon.

Two thousand years ago, a medium-sized earthquake had changed the flow of water by blocking the river and forcing it to go deeper. The rivers of molten lava had left underground tunnels called tubes that acted as conduits so the water didn't reach the surface. It carried the river underground until it reached one hundred miles south of its present site. There it burst free, creating a natural lake.

El Grande Gringo could not stand by himself unless he was standing next to a wall and he had his walking cane with him. He had to stand very still. He fell occasionally. Someone was always there to help get him up. Everyone loved him. Delores, the midwife, looked after him. She now had several aides. Bright, beautiful young women became her aides and helped her with El Grande Gringo and her clinic. After three years of experience with Delores, the aides could make trips on their own to see their patients. She was a good teacher. The well taught, experienced, competent aides were available day or night. The death rate in childbirths in their area was cut in half. The medicine given in the clinic offered people a chance for a cure they never had before. The clinic and the workers were spotlessly clean. A bigger clinic was opened. No one was ever turned down due to lack of money.

Mercado has one saloon and it was called La Cucaracha, which means "the Cockroach." It was well named. Nearly three months had passed since Ron's streak of luck ended with him rendered incapacitated. The first thing I notice upon arrival in Mercado is the sight of Ron's former horse, distinguished by its size and unique ashen color of gray.

I dismounted, and I noticed some people coming toward me. They were not threatening, only curious. I went inside the saloon. It was lazy-looking place until they saw me. My badge didn't help me any. I smiled and asked for a cup of coffee. The coffee was strong and blistering hot. I told the bartender, "It's the best I have ever tasted." I almost got sick a minute later. A big fat roach crawled out of the wet rag the bartender was wiping the bar with. The bartender squashed the bug with his hand, and parts of it flew all over the bar. One landed on my shirtsleeve. I didn't drink any more coffee.

The bartender smiled until I asked him, "Who owns the gray mare outside?"

A short man with his hat in his hands stepped forward. "He is mine. I found him."

I told him, "He is yours, indeed. I did not come for the horse. I am looking for the man who rode him. Did you see him?"

"No, I saw only the horse near the dry river. The horse did have blood on his fetlocks, a great bit of blood. The horse was not injured, so it had to be from someone or something else."

I told the old man and the others, who now had relaxed by now, "I am Tom Davis, the marshal of Santa Fe, New Mexico. The man who owned this horse is dead. I am giving this man a clear title to the horse he found. And two rounds of whiskey for each of you."

I had two choices. One was to go south of Mercado into Mexico and see if there was any sign of him. Or I could go to the San Miguel Mission and see if anyone had seen him or heard of him. I spent two weeks going south and had not one single clue where Ron could be.

I started back to where the dry bed of the river forked. I was a couple of miles from it when the rain started. It was a flash flood, wiping out all the tracks. I just missed being caught in the flood that was caused by the rain from a hurricane that came ashore on the Baja Peninsula.

Two days later, I rode up to the old mission. I had spent four weeks in Mexico looking for Ron. The adobe bricks making up the walls looked a little worn, and there were a couple of places that had to have been leaks in the past, but the old mission looked pretty good. The rain sealed the small gaps by running the mud from the bricks down into the cracks. All in all, it was doing well for its age. It had been over a month since I had seen Ron ride out of Phoenix. My sixth sense was silent. It probably meant Ron was dead. I walked into the mission. I bought a candle and lit it. It didn't hurt to cover all the bases.

Pablo saw me and came over. I explained why I was looking for Ron. Pablo told the story of how the Mendez family found El Grande Gringo and brought him to the mission for treatment. The money was never mentioned. El Gringo was on a pallet behind some blankets that had been hung up. Pablo led me around the blanket. My first glance with him lying on his side made me think it was Ron. Then I changed my mind. This stooped old man could not be Ron. He had to be older than Ron by at least twenty years.

I spent several hours just sitting there, watching the effect he had on the different types of people coming there to see him. He was as regal as a king. El Grande Gringo was quite a sight. He affected the people more than a king would have. There was an abundance of reverence surrounding the whole mission.

Although he never said a word or moved a muscle, he communicated with them. Once I thought I felt those blue eyes on me, but when I looked again, I saw no sign of life there. All of us there knew he was a man of God. I compared this man with Ron, who was six foot three and weighed 280 pounds. This man was less than six feet and weighed less than 240 pounds. His eyes were blue. Ron's eyes were brown. His hair was white while Ron's hair was brown. This man was a man of God. Ron was totally evil.

I leaned over, touched him, and said, "Sir, this is Tom Davis. I've come to take you back to Phoenix."

There was no twitch of his body or blink of his eyes. I knew right then my days of hunting Ron Jedrokoski were over. Whoever or whatever this man was, he was now a good man, a miracle of God. It was time for me to go home!

The San Miguel Mission and clinic kept growing. They put rails everywhere for El Grande Gringo to hold on to when he wanted to go outside. Someone walked on each side of him and helped support him. Everyone loved El Grande Gringo.

The room they had built him had a roofed patio outside his room so he could sit in the shade and feel the light breeze blowing through the patio. The two-and-a-half-foot-high patio walls gave his visitors a place to sit. And he did have visitors. The visitors came in droves, and soon the crowd of visitors got bigger and bigger. The patio was doubled. They would sit quietly, some for hours, waiting for their time with him. Most of his visitors felt God, using El Grande Gringo, would grant their requests. El Grande Gringo became a shaman, a holy man. The shaman of the Apache had also been a holy man.

The advice of El Grande Gringo was sought by everyone even though he only grunted. He became a holy man even though he could only nod his head. His advice always seemed to be good even though he never spoke. He seemed to make a lot of people well just by them touching him. The word spread. The crowds increased. The San Miguel Mission buildings and the town grew rapidly.

Another minor miracle occurred. Tito was repairing a broken board inside the mission when the board pulled free. An embroidered cloth banner fell out of the area being repaired. The cloth was undamaged. He opened it up and saw a message on it. To his amazement, he could read it even though it was written in Apache. Pablo said it was in Comanche. Delores thought it was in the Pima Indian language. "The Lord's Prayer" was captioned on the banner, and everyone who saw it knew that this is what it said:

> O Great Spirit, you are our Shepherd Chief in the most high place. Whose home is everywhere, even beyond the stars and moon. Whatever you want done, let it also be done everywhere. Give us your gift of bread day by day. Forgive us our wrongs as we forgive those who wrong us. Take us away from wrongdoings. Free us from all evil, for everything belongs to you. Let your power and glory shine forever. Amen.

I, being a shaman, could normally see into the future. I couldn't see Ron or any trace of him in my visions. It meant Ron probably no longer existed. He must be dead.

The traffic going through the mission increased. Almost all of them wanted to see and touch the one called El Grande Gringo. It seemed the ones in the clinic who touched him healed quicker than those who didn't touch him. He made everyone feel better. He never turned anyone down. People came from miles around to talk to him although he couldn't answer. A nod of his head was enough.

Money began appearing in the mission's alms box. It was almost enough to break even. The second project was the well. When they dug it out, the water was sweet again, and they had enough water to share. The Gila River was only fifty yards from the mission building now. It never ran low.

Pete, a blacksmith-metal worker, opened a business one hundred yards from the mission.

The small mercantile store in Mercado moved to San Miguel, tripling their business. Eggs and chickens and all kinds of other items of barter were accepted just like money as payment to the merchants. Almost all the people grew vegetables since they now had enough water. Bartering made sure everyone had enough to eat. Ladies making dresses, blankets, and shoes took over the next patio built by the mission group

The money coming in kept increasing. Three rooms were added for the Mendez family. Two rooms, one with a confessional booth, were added for Pablo. Delores got three rooms for her clinic on one side of the mission, including separate doors to her clinic. She got two rooms for herself on the other side of the Mission. Then they added two classrooms and two dorms. Although El Grande Gringo's money was down a little, it would soon be back where it had started. They still had most of it. The mission building size was doubled with pews added. Then they doubled it again. It kept growing in leaps and bounds. The one-room mission was now the biggest mission church in the New World. Everyone thought El Grande Gringo had brought it to this stage. And maybe he had.

Pablo, Delores, and the Mendez family believed it. The pope heard about Pablo and made a special designation for him. He was called "the Faithful One," and that was his name from then on. The pope declared him a priest. He became Father Pablo, the priest of San Miguel.

Delores's medical clinic became famous for its special treatment of the sick and diseased. Famous doctors, surgeons, and specialists took their sabbaticals here. Their service was free, and most of them donated substantial sums of money to the clinic. It became a model college of medicine called the San Miguel Hospital of Hope. It was dedicated to Delores.

Six months after saving Ron's life, the Gonzalez family was recognized for their lifetime of care and maintenance of the old mission. They were awarded a house near the old mission and allowed to do whatever they wanted to in the mission. Tito and Juanita started caring for old people, and the mission ran a model assisted-living center. Professional care workers had their own school and dorms. Tito and Juanita's daughter became one of the most famous female surgeons in the world, while their son died in San Salvador working with the sick that had contracted some diseases never before recorded, such as the Ebola virus. He was asked to join many medical teams who went all over the world studying new diseases with no total cures before he became a research project volunteer himself. The disease discovered in San Salvador and named after him created such high fevers that almost everyone who contracted it died before it could be identified.

By the end of his life Ron, El Grande Gringo, had been responsible for more good than evil. God used him in many ways to help bring peace, love, and light into their lives.

Printed in the United States
By Bookmasters